A FINE DAY WILL BURN THROUGH

Stories

William Auten

FIRE IN HAND MEDIA

A Fine Day Will Burn Through
First edition
May 2021
©2021 William Auten

ISBN (print): 9780578866567
ISBN (ebook): 9780578866604

Published by Fire in Hand Media
Fire In Hand Media colophon is a registered trademark of Fire In Hand Media LLC
fireinhand.com

CONTENTS

A FINE DAY WILL BURN THROUGH

Stories

FOMO

Today at ten in the morning, Mr. Snickerdoodle isn't having much to do with the scenery, commotion, and the crew and props passing back and forth in front of him. Neither his tawny eyes nor his ear tufts can keep up—at least not where he sits, stressed out, having plopped on his rear end in protest, tail convulsing, dropping down onto the dusty floor, the smoke-black tip never touching the ground, tail sharply rising again in a spasm whenever voices shout, wheels squeak, metal clanks metal, or another backdrop painted like an evening rattles by.

With Studio Six freezing and the warm mid-morning sun, in which he would lounge at this time of day, sealed off, Mr. S isn't up to snuff for his shoot. His paws have navigated debris on the ice-cold concrete he's never felt or smelled. The green-yellow artificial lights surrounding him hum and buzz like a sick moat. Static hovers over him wherever he retreats in the room—and then retreats from his retreat. Bit of a confused mood he's in, which is hard to discern because his face is perpetually frozen in a state of adorably smashed confusion. His cooperation skills smolder—not the level of amenable warmth his trainers promised in the contract. The turquoise-inlay bolo tie looped around his neck isn't helping the situation.

For about twenty minutes, Mr. S. has preened and pranced around the outside of the communal litter box until, finally, Ken clued in on the number of Mr. S.'s drive-bys on his vanilla-caramel-ice-cream-swirl legs under the edges of Ken's phone and his refusal to step into the litter box's spots sans lumps, of which there are several because Karen scooped it clean after the first round of filming involving Mr. S.'s co-stars, who weren't any more excited to be here but were more willing to participate in what pays the bills and puts food on the table for Karen and Ken and keeps employees, such as Mr. S., off the streets, out of the shelters, and away from irresponsible owners as well as from population control.

By 10:37, Ken places a separate and private litter box for Mr. S. off the soundstage, away from lights and cameras, at the back of the filming area and near the food table and napkins, plastic cups and utensils, and omnivore, vegetarian, and vegan options. "Don't worry," he says to the catering coordinator's passive-aggressive protest. "He probably won't touch it. Fish is more his thing. He had breakfast before we left."

The golden Chinchilla Persian looks up at the catering coordinator as she tries ignoring him and slides a tray of red-dusted deviled eggs and deli meats away from the table's edge and his line of sight. She glances down at Mr. S. again. Perpetual sad and adorable look in return from the cat. The catering coordinator's hip taps the tray a little deeper into the middle of the table.

Keeping his uninterrupted look of natural bewilderment on his face, Mr. Snickerdoodle cocks his head at Ken, casting his eyes up at the animal wrangler, and sinks his head toward the litter box before stepping into the litter like a sharp-dressed passenger squeezing in between two drunks on the subway for the last available seat on a long ride home.

"See?" Ken says, smirking at Mr. S. "Not so bad, you little sh…" Ken cuts off his own profanity-laced response as he chokes on roasted turkey and sharp cheddar sandwiched by brownies.

It's still early in day one of the next episode in this new direct-to-web series, the bulk of it to be filmed before noon when all the animals involved—human and feline—can focus better, but the two-and-a-half hours have been long for the two-person outfit of Push Paws, one of Hollywood's leading supplier of animal actors.

"I can see why Dad got out," Ken mumbles as his sister, on the soundstage and handling some of the other cats, seethes at him. After wiping food from his mouth, Ken chases his snack break with a few gulps of coffee and tongues any remaining food from his front teeth before clearing his throat and, one last time, eyeing Mr. Snickerdoodle, who chases himself in the litter box, unable to land on a spot available only for him. Ken taps the box with the toe of his sandals.

Smashed-face confusion as a response from Mr. S. who stops following the end of his own tail and tracks in the sand and looks up.

"Don't go anywhere." Ken throws away his napkin, hikes up the belt to the underside of his belly, and stuffs a water bottle in the back pocket of his khakis before walking back to where the film lights end and the next scene waits to begin.

The director with round glasses and a ponytail emphasizes this shot needs to be treated like it's another day, another dollar at the rollicking saloon a few blocks off Main Street and near Miss Citronella's brothel and the boardinghouses for the migrant workers that, as the digital series unfolds, Mayor Thelma set up for the hard-working cats new to the area, its hills filled with silver and opportunity, but unfortunately continues to attract dogs of all shapes and sizes, led by a French bulldog named Butterball.

For the upcoming interior shot of P.H. Ticklebottom's saloon, Karen tries to get LC (Lil' Concordia) positioned at the end of the old-timey piano where Prescott, swiveling slightly on the stool, scatters his yellow eyes back and forth across the horizon, waiting for what will be his cue to slide his fat orange head down the keys in the middle of a Stephen Foster classic, marking most of the ivories with his scent in one swoop. Karen motions to Ken, who waves back to his sister. She waits for him to put down his phone, which he does and slowly steps onto the set, picking up his pace when he makes eye contact with her. "Get them, please. We're ready," she says, softening her voice with him, as she throws her sweaty forehead toward the two kennels behind her.

Backlit by the soundstage lights, her five-foot-ten, Art Garfunkel–haired brother, who's into TRX sessions down at PCH Athletic Club, where they have yet to give him the results he wants, sighs, unglues his finger from his phone, stalls on his way to open the first kennel, phone still in hand, and sighs again, cheeks puffing out, as he puts away his phone and opens the first kennel's and then the other kennel's gate until the two shorthairs —one shaded silver with amber eyes and the other, a calico—can scamper out and stretch before Ken wrestles them in position at one end of the bar, placing their hats, vests, and badges on top of the bar crowded with a cigar, a deck of playing cards, and a few shot glasses topped off with watered-down cola. He loads the toy plastic guns with a smoke emitter handed to him by the propmaster—the second pair of guns after Ken cracked the hammer of the first while fast-drawing the plastic revolvers and snickering, "Draw, you mangy varmint!"

Watching her brother stumble with the work she's asked of him, Karen glowers before steering to a positive image she's clung to since earlier this year. Thinking about singing some of her favorite rock songs eases where she is, who she's with, and where she has been the past few months—this image of her swaying on a stage in front of a crowd and, awash in a spectrum of colored lights, having dusted off her devil rock-horns and polished her voice, which last made an appearance at Tweety's Thursday night karaoke before her son became quiet and solitary.

Deputy Hamburger, sliding from Ken's arms like wet pizza dough onto the saloon's moon-lit floor, rips apart Karen's image of belting an outro chorus. "Come here, you little…" Karen hears her brother curse as he scrunches the scruff of the calico and slings the unhappy feline tornado into the middle of the saloon.

"Fiver!" Ken shouts to her, walking off the stage, opening a bottle of hydrogen peroxide, and whipping out his phone while dousing his bleeding hand.

Karen inhales deeply and exhales deeper because she would love to step off the soundstage and have one of her brother's incessant breaks—several already this Monday morning. Her brother's fivers are mainly to catch up, he swears to her, on his job searches, but Karen knows it's mainly his dating-app profile because not only has the financial well gone dry for her brother but also the romantic well. She needs to bring up the amount of time he spends on his dating app, and at the TRX studio, for which she has agreed to pay because she can't afford to pay him a salary, and the lack of time he's spent searching for a job in the recovering real-estate market, perhaps getting his old one back at Valley Homes. He helps with Russ and at work until she cleans up their father's accounts and sells Push Paws or until Ken lands on his feet.

But Chuck isn't helping. Ken has talked nonstop about his buddy Chuck who encourages Ken to be "so honest, so real" with his dating profile that no lady would swipe left and this brash confidence would unleash Ken's desired effects in the most important areas of his life—"all of them," according to Chuck. Which area, exactly? Karen has said to herself, rolling her eyes because the advice, which Ken seems to be tightrope-walking blindfolded, is from Chuck; Chuck whom Karen has known when he and Ken started hanging out together as freshmen in high school and have not separated since, both boys reaching their respective and yet shared peaks, topping off circa the state football quarterfinals against Ventura High twenty years ago and at the season-ending party at Tío Loco Tacos; Chuck whose sole purpose in life, then and now, is "to make bank" and "keep my metab crazy up." At one stop in Karen's life, putting up with the antics of her younger brother's friends was endearing, but the years have refashioned her innocence, and she refuses to accept the age wrapping around her, pressing her tightly until the colors of life in front of her pall.

But Chuck's advice has stuck with her since she heard it from Ken shortly after he had to move in with her and Russ. "So honest, so real." But with the sounds of high-octane singing and electric-guitar solos in her head dying out, she wants more than a fiver to catch her breath after all the four-legged wrangling, hair balls, meowing, and in one corner of Studio Six right before filming started, a cat-on-cat accident involving Mick Jagger and Leo—the two big-boy velvets who don't put up with anything or anyone especially when they are in the same room. Gray hairs spread in her head, and these grays smother the image of her singing on stage.

"You OK?" she forces through a smile, mouthing it to Ken as a cutout full moon on a painted night sky with baying coyotes rolls behind her.

Ken's bandaged thumb lifts before he returns to his phone.

Walking back to the soundstage, her sleepy-eyed brother dresses Deputy Hamburger, looks over him once more, and after Karen's gentle nudge, apologizes to the cat while he creases the calico's collar and loops the gold watch on the vest's buttons. The good deputy yawns straight ahead into the lights. Ken rests Sheriff Pantaloons's paws on the toy gun's handle. Ken takes pictures with his phone, snickering at the silver-shaded polydactyl ready to smoke the six-bullet wheelhouse holstered low on his hindquarters.

"Is he good to go?" Karen motions to the furry spot circling, stopping, circling in the litter box near the catering table. She tightens her two knee pads and kneels behind the bar, prepping the area where Mr. S. will stand while Ken or Karen move his front leg back and forth over the bar, washcloth in one paw, sliding a mug with the other.

Ken shrugs. "Yeah, I think so." Aiming Sheriff Pantaloons's other toy gun at the saloon's fake-wood floor, he looks down the sight and grumbles gunshots, quaking his lips as the aftershock.

"You *think* or you *know* so?" Karen swipes gray hairs off her face, dragging sweat and makeup. She digs out a smile and offers it to Ken.

"I'll check." He pushes up with the help of the bar, knocking it out of place, exposing the L-shaped masking tape underneath. He waddles over to the catering table and the private litter box where Mr. S. has not deposited anything.

When the bar screeches across the floor, the director looks up from his laptop, the mauve lenses of his glasses bouncing up and down, his ponytail swaying, and radios in. "We need Props…again." He stares at Karen before returning to his keyboard.

Behind the bar, Karen swallows hard and flops down, close to crying but not wanting to. Her teeth have quickly accumulated another yellow coat from the amount of coffee she has consumed and the time she hasn't made for brushing them. But she has made time for this production and its demands and prepping for it the last days, mostly on her own, though Ken was present, lounging in a chair in Push Paws' office, helpful when asked to help out but not helping on his own. She's poured all she has left into the business she inherited from her retired parents, struggling week by week to pick up more opportunities, while also dealing with Russ's evolution from isolation and withdrawal from all social activities at home and school a few weeks ago to bruising his classmates; he started with pinches on the face but has, according to his fourth-grade teacher, moved to "other parts of the body." Ms. Gutierrez and Karen agreed, all other factors remaining mostly constant in Russ's life, the death of Marcus must be the root.

Karen decided to put down their cat, but she wanted Russ to be part of a family decision. She wanted him to understand Marcus had a good life, but it wasn't the same for him anymore, and the things he loved to do with Russ and the things Russ loved to do with him—purring, lap-sitting, playing with string and a catnip-loaded ball—faded. She explained "quality of life" as best she could. She repeated what her father emphasized the first time she said goodbye: "One of the family," not merely a pet. But she altered his other words, placed their meanings and sentiments on Earth, nowhere else, not above, as she had believed. Russ nodded and ran away, slamming the door to his room. Uncle Ken put down his phone and knocked on his nephew's door.

That night she thought of her father who had told her animals are not afraid to die. "We need to help them when they're at that point," he said as the two of them stood over the body of her first cat. She was a year younger than Russ, and she asked her father about heaven for animals, the souls of animals, what the Bible says about animals; about God and Jesus and the animals. "They'll be there waiting for us," her father answered before kissing her on top of her head. Idling in the vet's parking lot, they laughed. Her father retold the old family joke about how Fergs, when he was a kitten, was supposed to be a dirty-snow-white cat, but he couldn't shuffle off his tabby coat in time. They were stuck with him that way because he was stuck in it.

And sitting behind the bar of a saloon filled with cats, dressed in period costumes, meowing and hissing and surrendering to the faux-wood floor, and the grunting sounds of two beefy props guys pushing the bar back onto the L-shaped masking tape, the gas lamps inside the saloon flickering on and off, and the cutout moon on a painted sky rolling into place behind the saloon's front window, the image asking Karen to step out of this infinite gray maze is the upcoming trip to Dave Duvall's Rock N Roll Fantasy Camp. But it quickly fades, loses its bright colors. She would let everything in front of her unwind: her brother, her son, the two-month contract to work on *Old West*

Cat Town keeping the family business and the thirty-year legacy of her parents vibrant. One part of her wants to follow the string leading out of the neutral-colored maze enclosing her. But another part of her knows she should stay where she is—as a witness to ordinary days.

If she could, she'd let this all uncoil at the entrance of the camp she's been eyeing ever since Double D himself—older, bloated, less hair, less makeup and lip gloss—announced on his website the dates for his rock camp. SPACE IS LIMITED! SIGN UP NOW! And she did, listening on loop to Destination's "Chose or Lose," the power love-ballad MetalMemories.com says, "remains the one-hit wonder's biggest and best, and puts bad-boy Duvall's soft side on full display." The song bewitched teenage Karen—the tones and lyrics about corporal wishes; a red light diffusing in the shadows taking over.

Entering her credit card info, her pulse spiked that night, like it did the first time she secretly listened to this kind of music, the music seizing her, and she wrote a list of the songs she would perform—all banned when she was a teenager, except for one song and one band her parents approved. She had told Siri to make a new note reminding her of the dates for *Dave Duvall Rock N Roll Fantasy Camp*. Siri complied, saving the event as *Dave Dubai Rick Roll Camp*.

One of the gas lamps pops, causing the cats that hadn't already flopped to the floor during the break to army-crawl across the ground. Sheriff Pantaloons scampers into the kennel, and Prescott runs his fat orange head over the piano keys. Hand on hip and scratching his eyebrow, the director calls for a lunch break—Props to fix the lamp and all of production to regroup. He glares at Karen before grabbing his coffee cup, avoiding a row of tin-foil stars dangling between the nightscape and P.H. Ticklebottom's windows, and steps into the sunlight. The studio's metal door slam behind him.

Ken plops down next to Karen. "Whew. *L-o-n-g* day."

She closes her eyes as she exhales.

"You sticking with Maiden for your band camp?"

"I changed it, but it doesn't matter. I'm not going."

"You could totally stun them with 'Run to the Hills.'" He swipes an image on his phone. "That'd be so real."

Karen looks at her brother, looks away. "I was thinking about singing Stryper. 'Always There for You'."

"OK." He can't keep a straight face. "Cool."

"I like the lyrics. They're open." She stares at tubes of cats lounging and sleeping all over the saloon. "They can mean something different to each person."

"But they're not real metal."

"They *sound* metal."

"Power-pop-keyboard-watered-down metal."

"You're one to talk, Nickelback."

"They're *rock*, not *metal*," Ken quickly counters, thick thumbs punching away on the keypad. "But Stryper? That was when we went to church. It was the only thing they'd let us listen to." He cleans his phone's screen with his white Push Paws polo, dragging the portfolio of women closer to the logo of a dog, cat, horse, and lizard.

"Look them up."

"I remember what they look like. Sparkly. Way too clean. Bible verse everywhere you turned."

"No, the song. The lyrics. It's only 'you' and 'I.' Nothing else. Nothing preachy. Love, loneliness, the world closing its door. You can sing it to whoever. And the tune does jam."

After a few more minutes of selecting five women from his search results, Ken says, "You practiced so hard."

Karen watches Mr. Snickerdoodle drop double-duty in his own private litter box but continues circling himself, adorably remorseful and confused, because he can't figure out what to do with the turd clinging to his fluffy back leg.

"I heard you in the shower and in the car every morning waiting on me. You totally sound like Dickinson." Ken raises his fist in the air, voice in vibrato.

The director walks by them, flops his ponytail, and departs before Deputy Hamburger weaves his leg.

"You were crushing so much tea and honey. Your voice was so ready…so real." Ken swipes his phone. "If you change your mind and want to go, I'll watch Russ. I got all this." He motions to cats knocking over glasses and props. "You don't have to miss out. Chuck says…"

"Chuck says." Karen's voice blends into her brother's and fades with her smirk and an eyeroll as Chuck's online profile of him finger-gun-pointing to his lifted shirt and abs underneath appears in her head.

"Yeah. Making stuff so real, so honest, not missing out. They go hand in hand." He opens another tab and finds the music video and lyrics.

Karen remains focused on the gas lamps dimming in the saloon.

"Yeah. Good song. Nothing too heavy. I can see why."

Half-smiling, Karen stares into the false nightscape in front of her—a generic moon and generic stars shaped by generic hands. She sees in her bedroom her suitcase denting the mattress; lying there to be unpacked elsewhere; waiting to be moved in another direction. Hard-shell, navy blue bordering on black, a red collar buckled around the handle, next to her contact info, telling her it's not a stranger's but hers to take.

Corporate Games

R ed light on his GoPro clicks on, and with one glove held in the air, signaling time out, Jay adjusts his hat's bill and digs into the box on a 1-1 count with the mandatory courtesy ball and foul-strike each batter brings to the plate. The ump lowers his palm and points to the pitcher. The southpaw, who moves toward home like a flamingo slowly dropping a leg from its belly, arcs the softball toward Jay, whose pear-shaped head traces the ball's path with the camera perched atop him.

Watching from the dugout, Mel sees the pitch is not worth swinging at, and were it to land without an opposite force smashing into it, the miniature yellow sun of a ball would set snug between catcher and ump. But Mel knows Jay will swing, especially with the GoPro on and his white-collar-athlete persona cranked up—and he does but only at the late-summer air. The ump issues his final warning about bat control to the RiverTech team. The shortstop for Dyna-Stix Adhesives covers her face with her glove but not before Mel watches her chortle with the second baseman who opened the floodgates with a three-run double in the top of the first and smacked a two-run homerun his second time at bat in the same inning during the softball event at the Richmond Corporate Games.

"What time are you meeting her?" Gabby asks Mel.

"Seven."

"Dinner?"

"Maxine's."

"*Ni-ice.*"

Jay shakes out his ponytail until it covers HAMMER TIME on the back of his jersey, steps in the box on his 1-2 count, and thrusts all his weight at the next pitch—another big cut from the lead data architect at RiverTech. The ball squeaks off the bat handle and stops a few feet outside the pitcher's circle. Jay hustles down the line as much as his cubicle glutes and hamstrings allow, but the lanky logistics coordinator for the area's leading supplier of silicone adhesives picks up the ball and flicks it to first without breaking a sweat.

Mel sighs at Gabby who shrugs—the two of them the sole representatives from Finance. "She may stop by after some errands." He runs his hands through his hair's silver loops before massaging his wrist.

"Doug has yet to take me there. The two Mikes went there for lunch last Friday."

"Is that why they blew off our meeting?"

"Mike H. said it was the best roasted chicken and sweet potatoes he'd ever had. Real, homemade marshmallows on top."

"Smelled like they had a few drinks." Mel stands up from the bench and shakes his hips left to right, but the pain clings. He tries ignoring Jay who, standing outside the dugout, turns toward him and gives a big thumbs-up after Kaitlyn, one of RiverTech's UX designers, reaches first on an accidental bunt, surprising her and the opponents. Mel stares at the GoPro before looking away. He knows when the tournament is over Jay will edit the film and add a soundtrack from 1980s action movies as he has for the past two years. "I thought if things are going all right, we'd go for some ice cream at Short Pump Creamery."

"Is that all for dessert?" Gabby winks.

"I'm old."

"You never *kno-ow*. I'm happy you're doing this. It'll work out. It'll be good."

"Yeah, I guess."

"Ah, to be swimming in the dating pool again."

"I got twenty-five years on you. It's a little different for us old farts."

"*Thirty*-five or more, which puts me back at twenty-four, right?"

September's waning light shrinks the park's tree trunks. Gabby's son sits with her husband in the stands behind the dugout and on his hands as though he's disciplining himself, or has been told to, but his knees pump up and down; every few minutes his head twitches.

Mel nearly spits out his water when he sees Dylan. "Did he grow overnight?"

Gabby slides on her glove after the inning ends on a fly-out to the centerfielder. "He'll be a teenager by this time next year."

"Where have I been?" Mel stares at the awkward beanpole dressed in a wrinkled oxford, torn black jeans, and black Chuck Taylors and sitting close to the stairs where he could slip away without saying goodbye or hello.

• • •

A year ago, the James River chilled his legs and arms. Much time had passed since he ran on trails and longer since he ran for reasons other than getting his mind off things. Wheezing and slobbering on his shirt with the number 867-5309, Jay pulled back from the front of the group, not because Mel was slow, not because Jay was too fast and was being considerate, but because Jay scanned his GoPro camera down the line of his colleagues' sweaty, muddy, and shivering bodies heading toward the tire run and the wall climb. "There they are," he chanted, spitting out the *Chariots of Fire* theme song from his chubby cheeks. Mel happened to be at the rear, not because he was slow and not because he didn't want to go any faster. He wanted to run alone, but Gabby suffered and laughed next to him, which he appreciated. He knew the feeling of shedding his own skin and floating outside his body—a runner's high—was an illusion brought on by oxygen and blood.

During the team obstacle course, the day's confidence ticked up for the web-content creators and project managers. Jay wanted to put on a strong show for their first-ever participation in the Games. His emails and bullet-point announcements at meetings in the months prior appealed to the weekend runners and gym-rats or staff who mentioned being active or wanting to reach the much-discussed New-Year-New-You. Mel waited until the last minute to sign up and feared he was late, which might have been a relief, but Jay welcomed him to the fold, especially after he found out Mel had joined a gym with the company discount, PR'd in races, and placed in a few. "Age group. Top five or seven at most." Mel emphasized one Saturday morning arriving late for practice. "Not the whole thing."

The first part of the course wound around the banks of the James and through the woods, crossing by the old ammunitions factory and its burnt, ivy-strewn shell unearthed in sections. The falls were nearby, where the Powhatan had fished and washed their clothes, using the rocks as scrubbers and the river's natural suds. Mel knew this area well. He had run races through here and had beaten his pace every time. But this one— the relay with his still-new colleagues—was a starting-over.

His sister and his wife's family had wanted him to run The Komen. Gabby thought the same. "It might be good for you," she said. He didn't tell anyone he ran it. He showed up in the morning, sunglasses on, Atlanta Braves cap pulled low, and registered on the spot.

After the starting gun, he tried reaching a familiar groove in his breathing and stride on the road and with the other runners, but he never found it. He tapered into a jog that disintegrated into a walk. He had promised himself he wouldn't walk, but by mile two, he carried a different promise. More halfway before the finish line and the crowd, cheering and yelling, he slowed and shed his white shirt with the pink phrase IN MEMORY OF. He had a plain runner's top underneath. He folded his race shirt and, faking a minor injury, limped off the route. A few people stared, but no one asked questions or intervened. The day and its cloudless sky, the spring sun over him, charged his emotions. In their final months together, his wife no longer needed a bra for exercise.

But he refused to stop during the obstacle relay, and near a bend, his lungs and muscles burned the most, not from exhaustion or being out of shape but from pushing himself before he reached the transition area. As some participants passed him, Mel calmed his breath until he heard nothing but churning water and felt a cold patch of air near the building's foundry and the pit where Union prisoners were forced into labor. Small daubs of yellow and pink wildflowers grew within. Gabby waited next to Mel as the rest of the team sprinted for the tires where Jay tripped, face-planted in the mud, and throwing two stern rock-devil-horns in the air, popped up and wiped off his GoPro before barreling on—all of which fueled Mel, but he jogged in place. Arms in a V, Gabby rushed through the tires. Members from other teams, including Voodoo Economics, loaded with MBAs, chugged past Mel. But he surged across the obstacle and, running faster, caught up to where he had been in the pack and, holding the rear, helped his teammates scale a wall until the rope was free for him to pull himself up to and over the top.

Afterward, Jay knew of a downtown restaurant where specials for the corporate athletes awaited them. Mel opted not to celebrate the better-than-expected, nineteenth-out-of-twenty-two finish for the team. When he slipped off the monkey-bars portion of the obstacle course, straining his shoulder and ribs, nearly chipping his molars, lying prone in the mud, he planned on dropping out of the remaining events, which included an egg toss, team spirit, and tug of war—the grand finale. He lied to Jay that a friend needed help with something. Jay understood and, lowering his head, leveled his GoPro's cyclops eye to Mel's face: "Vaya con Dios." He couldn't tell if the camera was on. Gabby convinced him to come along.

They rolled into Penny Lane Pub to replace the carbs they burnt crawling through pipes, swinging on ropes, carrying large logs overhead, canoeing a section of the James, and running the equivalent of a 10-K. Mel limped around the pub and stopped in front of a plaque commemorating Liverpool FC's 1984 European Cup win. He used to have a mustache and permed hair like the player hoisting the trophy. Mel squinted at the club's badge and the motto crested in green above a red bird holding a branch in its mouth: YOU'LL NEVER WALK ALONE. He didn't know much about soccer, but he knew every piece of Beatles memorabilia crowding the walls. The albums, the magazines, the toys, the songs on repeat in the speakers seeped into him. He fought with his sister about sharing the record player. Mel liked the way Ringo tossed his head on the off-beats and the way Paul and George could sing and play when sharing a mic. He later understood why a smirk like John's could simultaneously pull in and push away.

"Damn it! That little…," Gabby grunted, glaring at a text and tightening her lips. "Dylan is up to no good again. I got to run." She told Mel goodbye and high-fived Jay and a few others on her way out.

"See you Monday," the chorus chimed.

Mel sat at the back of the group; no one paid attention to him. After a few minutes, he took one last sip from his pint, slipped money under the glass, and stepped outside into the courtyard designed to look like the entrance to a pub where the Fab Four would have played in their hometown, complete with signs for streets and the Underground, which neither weather nor time had worn down—those authentic and irrevocable details and voices familiar back then and again.

• • •

His bitterness about his dismissal from his previous job, the timing of it, and debating whether to sue for wrongful termination had faded. Mel heard that his replacement was part automated and part human—the former being software; the latter a woman fresh out of college. He believed he was let go because he was old and pricey, the topmost of middle management, settled, comfortable, not skilled enough, not diverse enough. But he found RiverTech on his own time and research and, he believed, earned the position based on skills and experience, which briefly boosted his morale because, during a follow-up interview, he re-emphasized to Gabby and the HR rep that he welcomed this chance for a new opportunity and new challenges and that he could bring more than what he had condensed on his résumé.

He met Dylan at his first RiverTech holiday party. Dylan was determined to destroy all the desks and computers and kick over all the trashcans before Gabby grabbed him. Mel noticed the energetic ten-year-old had a particular affinity for slamming expensive ergonomic chairs into cubicles, tearing down project schedules and calendars, and treating staplers like pistons.

As Gabby, white wine in hand, introduced Doug to her coworkers, Mel spied Dylan sneaking into the kitchen. Dylan's dad was tall, sported a square jaw and thick eyebrows, rigid—the complete opposite of the ball of energy jamming his cake-crusted fingers onto keyboards and flicking on and off floor lamps and surge protectors. The Navy officer had recently adopted Dylan, months after marrying Gabby. Captain Fernandez asked Mel if had kids. Mel shook his head no. The captain asked if he was married. He shook his head yes.

Excusing himself, Mel set down his beer near a laser-jet printer and walked the long aisle between management offices and chairs and desks arranged like dividers in boxes of chocolates. Everything was too quiet when he reached the trashcan and recycle bin sitting outside the kitchen. "Whatcha doing, buddy?" he asked, leaning against the doorframe.

The kid spun on his knees and faced Mel. He had found matches in one of the drawers. Bottom lip pushing out, eyes tearing up, Dylan frowned.

Mel put one of his hands on the kid's mop of chestnut hair and, with the other, reached into the top cabinet and pulled out an ordinary off-white candle. "I knew they forgot to get one of these out for the party. Good thing you got a light."

Dylan hugged his knees to his chest. His red, teary eyes looked up at Mel who nodded.

"Just one'll do."

An Incredible Hulk shoe toed the box of matches a few inches toward Mel's loafers. Sniffles and long stares spread from the kid to the new accounts specialist.

Mel fumbled with a few of the matches, unable to strike them. "Well, poo. I need some help. You know how to do this?" He made sure Dylan saw him run cold water from the kitchen sink on the used matches.

More sniffles and a stiff shrug from the red-and-green-striped shirt—snot drying on one of the sleeves.

Mel motioned Dylan his way and passed one match as smoothly as his arthritis allowed. "You got a steady hand. More than me."

Little brown eyes brightened with the quick flare.

"Lock and load!" Jay, beer in hand, bumbled his way into the kitchen. He had started growing out his hair and looked like a well-fed possum squeezing all he carries in the midsection into a camo jumpsuit zipped up one fourth of the way.

Dylan scampered off. Mel lifted the candle up and set it on the counter.

"Hey, we're going to Lazer Tag in a bit. You should come. It'll be *h-u-g-e*." Jay flashed his hand signals. "The Goonies win every year."

Many colleagues appeared with empty glasses and plates and congregated around them.

"No, you can't miss this," Gabby said to Mel, laughing. "I mean…right?"

Up the hill from the old farmer's market and the river's floodwalls, Mel followed the caravan of cars to a large industrial building filled with inflatable walls, barriers, fake shelters, and lights and sounds. "Tango-and-Cash time!" Jay yelled to a production assistant Mel had seen a few times but did not know. He only knew Jay and Gabby—one by name; the other he could trust. He held the plastic gun in his hand, stepped through the dry ice pumping into the first octagonal room, and found a crow's nest where he sat alone and could pick off the other team, if he wanted, which he didn't, or to defend himself, if he tried, which he didn't. He looked over ribbons of laser beams: What am I doing here?

• • •

Mel's knees creak and hands fumble for a bat near the on-deck circle as Gabby takes a final practice swing before entering the batter's box and sending a solid double over the head of the unassuming shortstop, putting a runner in scoring position.

"Bring her home!" Jay claps and rotates his tri-eye head over the diamond and park.

Mel settles in. The pitch from flamingo lefty floats, and it's a ball, too high, but Mel rips at the air. Strike two.

"Wait for your pitch," Jay says.

Grumbling to himself, Mel rewraps his hands around the handle. The pitcher steps forward from the mound, but his elbow locks against his ribs, causing his release point to drop below his shoulder. The ball emerges from the pitcher's left knee and revolves along a straight line that Mel's bat slaps, driving Gabby home. He stops halfway between first and second before retreating after the right fielder fires to second base. He clenches his hands until the stinging and swelling simmer.

No shutout—and the one run in pumps Jay and the rest of the team until Natalie from Marketing grounds out Mel and her in a double play, portending an imminent flood of offense from the two, three, and four batters on Dyna-Stix, two of whom Jay christened Hall and Oates On Steroids. And in the top of the next inning, Oates blisters a double to center right. Lower back flaring as he bends over, Mel bobbles the ball, which pops off his chest, but, keeping an eye on the runner, fires to the infield and stops Oates from advancing. Mel massages his collarbone and grimaces while his throwing arm burns and tightness spreads above his sternum.

Approving Mel's effort, Gabby smacks her glove.

He nods to her and clenches his jaw a little more. Dyna-Stix's shortstop singles, moving Oates to third, and sets up first baseman Hall who launches a three-run shot—his second of the day—over center left where Jay stops galloping toward the fence and ogles the homerun before it plummets near the duck pond and playground. After a few more solid hits and runs, Dyna-Stix ratchets up a 12–2 lead and pressures the ump to invoke the lead-by-ten mercy rule.

"You're going to have fun tonight. Knock her socks off or whatever she wants knocked off." Gabby slaps her glove on Mel's knee.

He smiles between apprehensive joy and physical pain.

"What does she look like?"

"Long hair, high cheekbones. Nice skin. Well preserved for a fifty-something woman. She said in her profile she was half-Korean. Born in South Carolina. Her dad taught at Clemson. Astronomy, which I think is pretty cool."

"Fifty-something? She doesn't say, or you don't know?"

"She had fifty on there."

"*Exactly* fifty?"

Mel shrugs.

"She lied about her age."

"You think so?"

"*I* would."

Jay calls for a pinch hitter when RiverTech returns to bat and continue the game.

A woman drifts by the first row of the stands; her eyes dart around the field and between the dugouts. She asks a stranger something. Her teeth are bright white, her clothes stylish.

She smiles and finds an open seat in the middle of the stands after the stranger points to RiverTech's dugout.

Lowering his hat, Mel sinks against the bench, blending in with the other uniforms.

Julie, a project manager, axes a nasty chopper into the dirt and is able to leg it out for a hit, keeping a rally alive long enough. Jay's voice cracks with hope.

Mel asks Gabby, "What are your plans for the rest of the weekend?"

"More than this?"

They laugh.

She bobs her head left and right. "Groceries. Some house chores. Probably will check work email."

Catcher Rick from HR scrapes out a single, moving Julie to second.

Jay wants everyone to stand up. "The pattern is *not* full yet, Ghost Rider!"

"Counseling is going better than expected," Gabby continues. "Even for having it on Monday nights, right after work for me and Doug." She inhales deeply. "My stress levels are improving. It's not the Patterson deadline." Her smile mixes politeness and grimace.

"Patterson may be my breaking point," Mel says.

The woman in the stands leans forward and looks up and down the RiverTech bench.

Mel slumps back against the dugout fence and looks at Gabby when she says Dylan admitted he wants to burn things, simply likes burning things, but not to hurt anyone or anything, like an animal, *ever*, he promised, breaking down in tears last week. Just to watch, he said, and he doesn't know why.

Coda

Their mother's email had its usual weekly updates—a general "Hiya Girls"—expected by the older daughter and had the same tone as previous ones: cheerful, informative, slightly dramatic, their mother, the Recorder of All Things Family and Neighborhood, commenting and observing the bland and atypical; who died; who was dying (cancer still the frontrunner, followed by cardiopulmonary diseases and dementia); whose offspring were doing good things in the world outside of "home" (but neither Debbie nor Harriet considered where they used to call home *home* anymore); construction in the area (traffic and petty crime encroaching like vultures); her flowers, her vegetables, and her desire for the recent weather to decide if the days are to be cold and frosty or behave more like spring; and the news that her month-long trip to Europe was happening—her knee-replacement surgery and sinus infection be damned. But the email's end, above their mother's signing off, jarred Debbie:

I've updated my LW&T (attached). Some changes. Won't have email at least until late after next weekend. I'll send pictures of all those quaint towns in the Old Country. Talk soon.

Love ya lots, Mom

Debbie opened LAST WILL & TESTAMENT OF PAMELA BEAUMONT TILLMAN, which read like the mortal version of the traditional wedding saying: Instead of something old, new, borrowed, and blue, the document listed things used, forgotten, unearthed, and filthy from dust and age. A year ago, their mother started giving away things; both daughters knew about the document since Debbie turned eighteen (her mother let her in on such responsibility if she "departed early"). Debbie tormented her younger sister, gloating as "Mom's executor." Pam and the girls discussed who got what. Fair and square, the document at the time claimed to be: Some things from their childhood; some things from their mother's life; some things that came to the family and from other lives decades ago; some things from when they lived together. Their mother changed the document over the years and let Debbie and Harriet know about changes but over the last few years didn't tell them anything, as though nothing had been changed—or, if it had been, it wasn't worth communicating.

The sisters knew some of the things they could inherit, sell, donate, or do whatever they wished with: books, clothing, knickknacks, furniture. Debbie and Harriet had agreed between the two of them that most of the furniture had no place in their respective lives, neither did the large handmade quilts from Amish in Kentucky nor the pottery picked up by their mother on a trip to Oaxaca. Artworks could go to a gallery, a museum, or an auction. The sisters did not commit to the things they could let go—except for the piano.

Debbie read the edited name, stopped, read it again. She double-checked the recipients: the email, like the previous weekly updates, went to Debbie and Harriet. She wondered why their mother sent this document before she left for her long trip—and why the recipient of the piano, upon their mother's death, had been changed from "Harriet Pamela" to "Deborah Anne, my firstborn." Of all the things Debbie expected to inherit, the piano was not one of them. Harriet had played and loved it more than when Debbie was her age. She had assumed a different outcome for it.

Standing there, towel-drying her face, Debbie reread the changes before going to bed. She wondered if she should petition her mother while, Debbie imagined, lounging with a glass of wine in a plaza; or if she should keep quiet about the change or until she and Harriet could talk. She checked her phone: nothing from Harriet, not that her younger sister had checked her email at the same time as Debbie. She started dialing but stopped. Harriet was out of town, not on holiday like their mother but with her company, and the results of the sales trip would carry her toward long-term permanent work or push her back into unemployment and uncertainty.

• • •

A pale artificial light washed out the conference room and the mostly filled seats. After Debbie greeted the students and asked them to confirm they were in the right place ("This is for your food handler's permit, not your driver's license or hunting, boating, or fishing…*or* jury duty."), most of the class chuckled; one person sheepishly stood up, gathered personal effects, and left, earning texting and low-key snickering from the back. Debbie looked around the room and was, once again, not the oldest person. Many of the students, she had noticed over the last few years, had been closer to her age than the typical teen or someone navigating quarter-life crises.

She started with the first lesson—the basics; the do's and don'ts of handling food and emphasizing county health codes. "Lawsuits aren't fun, and neither is losing your job because you didn't do yours." She flipped through slides and illustrations, stopping at every bullet point to offer more information, reasoning, and solutions. She tried not bogging them down in science, bacteria, viruses, and parasites, but she felt like she was teaching ninth grade biology again, her first job after college, repeating internal temperatures of chicken or beef and talking about communicable diseases, most of which were avoidable if simple instructions, such as washing hands or not sneezing over prep or cooking areas, were followed. She also knew they would not retain everything; most of them, after the class and test, would touch their faces and hair; and all of them wanted the passing grade and permit, which would transfer them from employees on probation to certified workers. She learned to have compassion and patience for the second- or third-timers trying again, often with the same employer. She knew who they were; she knew some of their stories. She did her best to make sure they all passed with minimum-needed knowledge.

As the remaining students returned to their seats, Debbie gathered the tests and, before heading to the office, told them to enjoy the free Wi-Fi. "I'll be back as soon as I can and get you out of here." She walked down the wing of the building where her cubicle, wedged in the middle, waited for her to hunch like a cobbler at a small desk.

Department supervisors had debated gutting the decades-old paper test and implementing an online version. But the debate had not ended, and Debbie remained responsible for a class of fifteen to twenty people, pencils to fill in answer bubbles, and a plastic box at the front of the room into which students dropped their tests. Were the online version ever to see the light of day, she assumed she would be in charge of it because of her institutional knowledge and experience, but she also wondered if doing away with the paper test and, she had heard the rumor, outsourcing the test to an online education-management company would redirect county resources and possibly her. And a computer, she knew every time she held class, could finish grading all the tests before she could.

After Debbie draped her sweater across the back of her chair, she checked her work email. The number of messages stamped with red exclamation points multiplied during class—messages asking for a link, an extension, or a quick turnaround on a renewal. As soon as she finished grading, she would deal with them, directing them with simple instructions on how to search on the website, thanks to a template she wrote years ago for a promotion. She laid the plastic answer sheet over the first test and, scanning down, pen in hand, marked the wrong circles punched out like new moons. She promised to return the tests before five and not keep the students in suspense until the next day or week—"Like when I started here," she told them. Her phone buzzed. Harriet was back in town, asked about drinks after work, but didn't mention celebrating, drowning sorrow, or something else.

• • •

"It was, like, embarrassing." Harriet scooted her lithe body closer to the table and whipped her hair into a loose bun. "Like, crickets." She wiped her eyes. "There was this video on loop next to me. All these different sports and people doing them. But no one stopped. Not a 'Hi' or 'This is interesting.' They just moved down to the next booth."

"I'm sorry."

"I'm probably unemployed."

"You don't know that."

"They won't keep me around after this." Harriet swilled the glass of rum and Coke and, pausing halfway, caught her breath. "I sat there at their stupid little booth, and no one did anything. I don't know what I did. I didn't have a mean look on my face. I wore makeup and had a nice suit. I was prepared. I had my script. I didn't get any names or anything. The next day Val said she got five names, and one of them was a group of angel investors. I'm done. I've got nothing to show other than one good month at the start of the year, and it's not enough." She fidgeted with her bun, wrapping and rewrapping until a few curly black hairs snapped. "I need something. I got bills. I need to feed my kids." She downed the rest of her drink, which shook her small frame and reddened her cheeks and collarbone; her eyes swelled again.

"What happened to the money I gave you to hold you over?"

"It got me through, but now with this…"

"OK," Debbie said after staring at Harriet.

They talked as though money was not the center where much began, pulled back, and reverberated. Groceries, utilities, rent, healthcare. They joked about Harriet ending up, as her one and last resort, back in fast food, where she started and made some headway as a young mother before she got in trouble again: The store manager would offer her either the breakfast shift (starting at three in the morning) or the dinner shift (lasting until eleven-thirty at night); childcare would be an issue for both shifts. They joked about Debbie passing Harriet again for the food handler's permit, as she had when no other options opened for Harriet. Some department colleagues knew Debbie had a sister but never knew what she looked like, and if the two sisters stood side by side together, the resemblance, save for the width of their frames, would bind them in plain sight. Debbie did not regret her decision to pass her sister, with the lowest possible grade, until Harriet quit the fast-food job a few months later.

After motioning to the waitress for a second round and a menu, Harriet asked, "Did you see Mom's email?"

Debbie raised her eyebrows over her wine glass and hummed.

"The one from Madrid?"

"I didn't know she sent that."

"She said she's not coming back…of course."

Debbie chuckled and wiped her mouth. "I'll have to read it." She fidgeted with her sweater's sleeves. "Did you see the one before she left? It mentioned the piano."

"What about it?" Harriet glanced over the menu.

"She changed her will."

"*Again?*"

"She's leaving it to me."

Harriet slammed down the menu and rummaged through her purse. "That piano is mine. I can't believe this. It's *mine*."

"She can't answer. She suspended her phone service for the trip."

Harriet cancelled her call, unwrapped her bun, and dragged her fingers through the top half of her head. "She knew I wanted it, and now she's taking it from me."

"I'll give it to you, Harriet. It's yours as soon as I get it."

"She *always* does this to me. Always. Like, I'm not good enough for something or whatever so she takes it away. Like she's judge, jury, and executioner."

"I don't know why she did it. She sent it with no explanation. You know how she is."

"And *there* it is." Harriet scrolled through the letter on her phone. "I can't believe her." Her boot heel pumped the table; her eyes narrowed like the end of a tunnel. "Damn her. I come back with no job and have to hear this. And then she leaves for

Europe, dumps this on me. Damn her. She had no right to do that."

"I will give it to you. I promise. I know how much it means to you. It's yours. It's not a problem." Debbie watched Harriet suck in her lips and spin through her phone. Her company, one of several start-ups in the county, produced shoes with built-in devices monitoring power, time, and speed. The sales force expanded last fall, hiring all levels of experiences and backgrounds and providing training for temporary assignments. They wanted the trade show to scale past the original consumer base of high-school athletes and into collegiate, semi-pro, and pro ranks. Ownership offered multi-level bonuses. Debbie encouraged Harriet to focus on the lowest level—two extra sick days and gift cards to restaurants in the area. Harriet had to acquire one new contact's name, email, or phone.

The two sisters had joked about shoe, dubbing the PlyoFire prototype "The Shoe From Another Planet" or, as Harriet squelched with a pretend radio in her hands, "Ground control to Major Tom, the shoe from Area Fifty-One is here. Live long and prosper, and may the Force be with you" because the training shoes looked like a reject from a special-effects company. A large saucer (flat but springy underneath its gray tarp) protruded from three-fourths of the toes; the rest (laces, tongue, heel) blended in like a regular athletic shoe and was veneer white except for the solar flares bursting along the sides and the company's logo (a pair of abstract calves outlined by flames). They looked heavy and cumbersome and like a waste of money, and to Harriet they were, but Debbie helped her tease out positives and practice the company's sales pitch. "It's more money than fast food," Debbie told her. Because of Harriet's time in rehab and jail and her dwindling options in the area, a job in another company would be hard to come by—no other doors lined the hallway Harriet had to walk.

Sliding her phone toward Debbie, Harriet said, "I think they only built less than a hundred of them. There's this gold plate on the inside with a production number and year. Eighteen-ninety-something. Either the Utica, New York, or Nashville factory." Her hands measured an invisible space smaller than a piece of bread. "Ours is in better shape. I mean, it has its dings and dents, but ours would be worth more. A lot more."

Debbie looked at the online auction site with the results of similar pianos and noticed the number of zeroes after the dollar signs.

• • •

The piano rested in a climate-controlled storage unit near the older, industrial part of town where their mom lived (an hour and a half, with good traffic, from them) and under a plastic tarp and soft cloths stitched together like a map. It was an upright with two silver rests for candles flanking the heavy wood frame;

latticework wove around the frame, down to the pedals and minor scuff marks that buffing and new stains couldn't cover. At first glance, it looked like any piano built in the late 1800s. Debbie and Harriet's great-great-grandmother played it in church, and upon her retirement, the music minister gifted it to her, which is when she handed it down to her daughter, and so on—one of the family dramas becoming which daughter, if there were more than one, and often there were, would inherit it. The songbooks and hymnals that came with it were long gone (foxed and crumbled), as was the original bench—the blue fabric worn to the point as though the sky was pulled apart thread by thread. Some of the keys barely reflected light in what had been a pearl-like surface. The sisters had thought its sounds were more powerful at night, after their mom's house had quieted; the notes on the higher register fell between a clock's echoing chimes or raindrops falling on glass. All that was missing, the sisters pretended, was a tormented, hypersensitive, and shy genius helming the keyboard.

Practicing was a chore to Debbie, and unlike Harriet, she never quickly picked herself up whenever a song's passage tripped her. Her younger sister, not a maestro but also not a novice, become monastic when playing, denying anything outside the songs she practiced until she was capable of repeating them without sheet music. She rolled her eyes and fluttered her eyelids when her hands shimmied over the keys, as though she were possessed and released music from within a centuries-old catacomb filled with cobwebs, stone, rats, and the beauty of slow decay. Spending time with the piano briefly shielded Harriet from the arguing and yelling growing between their mom and her; shielded her whenever Debbie could not be mediator or messenger anytime Harriet opened a door to something other than music.

Weeks after their mother returned from Europe, Debbie called; jogged with her through updates, gossip, and some events from her trip, such as nearly missing a connection when dairy cows crossed a railroad in central France; and waited for the right moment. "Would you give it to me now?"

"Before I'm dead?"

"Yes."

"Why?"

"Harriet loves it."

"I gave it to you, Debbie, because you understand those things." There was a long pause. "She's in trouble again, isn't she?"

"Yes."

"The shoe thing."

"They let her go."

"Is she going to hock it?"

"No, she's not."

After another long silence, Pam said, "You can have it now, but I don't want to know what you do with it."

Debbie anticipated her mother adding that request, and her anticipation unnerved her at first, and then it faded as she agreed with it and joined her mother in silence because her mother knew her daughters as intimately as Debbie knew her younger sister and herself; because she knew that the request—and the implication beneath it—wasn't anything new from her mother but that its single exact beam cut through the surface and backlit the roots below.

• • •

After work, Debbie waited in her car outside the storage unit. The sky was a brilliant blue, and the sunset was later than the day before, spring having deepened. The potential buyer was on his way to look at the piano. In the back-and-forth emails he seemed willing to buy it sight unseen, at the price Debbie had posted, but wanted to measure its dimensions in person in case it couldn't pass through his basement door; he mentioned bringing tape to mark the ground. Nothing signed, they had a verbal agreement, and Debbie printed off a Bill of Sale she had revised after searching for it in one of the databases at work. She eliminated all references to the Department of Health – Food Safety Division, the county, the state. It was a simple document, one that she probably could have found online or created on her own, but she had time between classes; finalizing it took less time than she had set aside. The potential buyer told Debbie that the piano would make a great addition to his growing collection of antiques; he thought that, once refurbished, it had "lots of potential."

As she sat there, the storage unit's door up, she wondered if something else that hadn't been considered or used in a long time was somewhere—or if items of various values could be strung together, their amounts adding up and ready to correct past gaps or inevitable future ones. She wondered if her house or garage buried this string; if the storage unit's other contents hid it; if the nooks and crannies of Harriet's small apartment held it. Debbie's eyes did not express *Once more, for old time's sake* as she looked at the piano's shape: a rectangle the color of the sky held in place by bungee cords and cloth ties. It didn't take much for her to imagine a sound resembling a xylophone in need of tuning —not a piano with the price at which it was about change hands. No other musings emerged.

A large red truck pulled in through the gate. Debbie watched it take the long way around to access the unit's door—if this truck was for her. Stopping at a row of units on the other side, it wasn't, and she leaned back in the seat and waited some more, feeling in that moment she was neither a sister nor a daughter and unrelated by blood, genetic traits (that extra mound of cartilage a quarter of the way up from the tips of their noses), or memories. Waiting in that moment for another moment to supersede her decision, she was not a liar or a traitor, though those feelings had jostled her, but she knew what the piano had been, many years ago, to her mother, sister, and herself (more to Harriet); and she knew where Harriet had been (where she started from, how she got there); and she knew what the piano was currently to them (all three of them) and where Harriet currently was (how she would wait for Debbie running toward her with a solution, as she had before) and what the piano and Harriet were never going to be.

She double-checked the lock on the unit's door, started the engine, and drove off.

Fog

Over the flatiron building, the fog drifts not like a poet's cat on soft feet but like the downy white hair or beard of God in popular cartoons of long ago, as He is still depicted from time to time—even in this time of recycled outrage wherein recent thinking has mostly freed us, like cotton in the wind, from anything of the past, these feelings turning us into idols, far from the alchemist's ancient dream of making gold from Earth's common things, such as the seeds of who *we are inside*, not what *we are to be*, billowing at the tips in full bloom like a tree carried from one place to another and replanted often in different weather from where it originated and thrived under certain conditions, this new rhetoric bypassing the old idea of the inevitable return to dust, life pulverizing and equalizing us all in the end—which reminds me of a joke my friend told, the punch line grown from centuries of tragedy and comedy and is more of a lesson hiding like a warm-feathered bird in cold-crusted bushes, which my friend Ethan told me is the root of Jewish humor, the joke's opening starting off how once there was a young man who had his bar mitzvah, "Stop me if you've heard this one before,"

my friend paused to chortle with happy-hour drink in hand, and
Ethan, his yarmulke crowning his head, turned to the crowd, and
I don't remember if the young man in the story is named the
same as my friend, but he is here because Ethan is a good name
from the Old Testament and the original covenant between God
and Man, this bond justifying ways not seen through a selfish
cloud, so go pieces of this phrase from a book written by a blind
Protestant poet whom no one reads anymore for various reasons,
such as his daughter improving his manuscripts when he could
no longer see, and Ethan in the joke sighs, but it's not a smug
sigh, as though he has something to prove to everyone who has
nurtured him with gifts, love, and support, but his sigh says
*Something is weighing on my shoulders and in my heart, and I need to say it
—I need to be me*, which is an expression he would confess today,
were he seeing this part in himself, but those older Ethans, both
of them, the one in the joke, the one telling the joke, said this to
me when I had a four-walled job and everything appeared
guaranteed, and Ethan looks at his family and friends, especially
the cute girl he has a crush on, whose floral dress and angelic
smile throw him off for a second, and says, "Thank you, but…"
and staring down the rabbi, says, "I don't believe in God," his
voice squeaking because he has hit puberty, but he recovers by
emphasizing the monosyllable of the Unspeakable Holy Name,
the microphone echoing his pronouncement and dragging it
across the auditorium, like thorns on roses, to which his

grandmothers, both of them, gasp as they should, as would my Christian grandmothers were I to say such a thing, which I once did, many years ago but to my father who folded the newspaper, nodded, and told me to clean up for dinner because my mother had worked hard in the kitchen preparing the meal, something she loved and wanted to do for my sisters and me, and for me to show up without respect and thanks, a lack of honor, was inconsiderate and self-absorbed, when I had started weeding out religion from my life at seventeen after reading about so much to deconstruct in the world around me, and Ethan is confident but not cocky, sweat forming on his pale skin underneath his black curls, and his father blusters, "We're having a talk after this," and his mother, confused more than concerned, says, "Ethan, what exactly are you saying?" and Ethan looks at Rabbi Davidovich, which, at the time my friend told me this, I didn't realize the surname referred to the son of David, the son of a Biblical character whom the Lord chose to be more than what he started out, little shepherd boy with a gift for music who defeated Goliath, a metaphor still used today for all the giants standing in the way to be killed, and by this act the rustic boy became king, this king sinned, the sinner repented, and the Rabbi responds to Ethan, who waited for a response from the middle-aged man from under whom Ethan has figuratively pulled the rug, this tall and plump teacher dressed in black and wearing a scarf, which I know is symbolic and has a Hebraic name, but I, for the life of me, can't recall but can see the pattern and colors in my head as clear as a path winding through a forest backlit by the sun, and Rabbi Davidovich smiles, but it's not a friendly smile, nor is it a smile to put the newly minted teenager in his place, but it is a smile cushioning what has been delivered, this revelation cutting into the main trunk of belief, a no-teeth-lips-pressed smile acknowledging a personal and local but not universal truth, and Rabbi says, "Do you think God cares?" and I remember chuckling with my friend Ethan and clinking our beer bottles, complaining about the Cardinals' bullpen, and talking about which of our office colleagues were not three-dimensional outside of their cubicles, and how he was going to temple for Passover and I considered Mass again, both of us admitting our decisions were based on the emotions of holidays and blood relatives from whom we cannot run, did not chose, and must love the person but not approve their actions, those few days with family when disagreements are set aside for a little while, like rabbits calling a truce from ransacking vegetable gardens, from what they naturally cannot help but do, and all this talk of ours unfurled in the bottom half of the country where, Ethan said, the Tribe wandered to, laughing as he did, and though it never parted down the middle for them, crossed the Mighty Mississippi like our common hero Twain who had spent time in California during the Gold Rush, commenting how a mine is nothing more than a hole dug by a gambler for the naïve to pay for, and who said, "The coldest winter I ever spent was the summer in San Francisco," but I don't know if he ever mentioned the fog, which probably was merely called fog back then but now has been classified by scientific observation and eagle-eyed inquiry as layers of vaporous phenomenon between air, land, and water, which doesn't diminish the dream-like effect of walking into it in late afternoon or, before it descends, under it, like a shadow surrendering whatever it has disguised, what anyone below or within can feel at certain times when basic elements reemerge from where they had been taken and held for so long in the sky, in plain sight.

Sun on Snow on Mountains

Passengers meandered from the station's various levels and drop-off zones, rode escalators and elevators, and gathered near times posted on digital clocks. Voices from overhead speakers updated repairs to tracks and stops between downtown and the imperial palace and reminded everyone to be vigilant for suspicious activity. Briefcases clicked on the floor, phones were checked, and young men and women in business suits finished their breakfasts. The sun brightened as it slid between canopies and parking garages to the south, and no one standing on the platform noticed the sunrise more than Mr. Matsumoto, who had witnessed similar repetitions during his years commuting to the office, but who, when he saw it, could not avoid looking at it— not yet at its highest or strongest and not physically or atmospherically different than any other sunrise.

A major decision for his company rested in his hands, but for the first time in a long time, family was more on his mind than business. He had stood on the platform at the same time for many years, waiting for the 8:45 to roll in and whisk him to the station less than two hundred yards from his office, where he would finish the morning commute with a stroll to the revolving front door while, as he walked, the mountain range grew in front of him and overtook the large glass building shining in the morning. He had seen these mornings when winter transitioned to spring, and he was familiar with the mountains' ridges, especially when sunlight emphasized them, like cuts and wrinkles on a giant animal hide, and the long rows of cherry blossoms lining the parking lot and sidewalks. Only a few times did he stop in one of the skyways connecting the offices to the factory and saw the sunrise as it brightened the basin. The sleek oval structure housed his office and shielded most, but not all, of the updated-for-the-sale factory stacked like goliath gray blocks on top of each other and accentuated with snaking pipes and the whir of turbines and chimney steam. In the early days, small engines had been assembled, all by hand and with tools perfected by his great-great grandfather and uncles, in a metal and wood shack later razed; industrial-sized engines, fabricated and quality-checked by computers and robots, now dominated the company's portfolio and caught a competitor's interest.

There was a time when the sunrise would not have mattered to him—it would have been a small, brief thing noticed before dismissed by him; there was a time when these small, brief things along his route from home to the station to the office would have been nothing more than backdrop. For all his hours spent with the sun, it had asked nothing of him, and he had asked nothing of it—not a prayer, a wish, or general tidings. There was a silent, mutual agreement between the two of them as they went about their day, each finishing tasks without the other needing confirmation; the sun rose until it reached noon and sank behind the mountains—this cycle without theatrics—while Mr. Matsumoto attended meetings or brainstormed with his teams inside the offices. He understood something out there was larger than him, something amateur and professional scientists, astrologists, and artists described as either dry enough for someone like him to grasp bare data and facts or meant to open the Great Cosmic Eye inside every person and see beyond statistics and measurements until the heliocentric universe wasn't *the* center but was *a* center among radiant points, depending on the vantage point—points becoming centers; centers becoming mere points—and depending where the recipient stood on the various planes crisscrossing and interlocking the universe. He understood this premise but didn't let it occupy him until he saw the sunrise.

Darting in from the outer wards of Kyoto, the silver train rolled into the station, whooshed to a soft stop, and slid open its doors. Before stepping in, Mr. Matsumoto glanced once more at the sunrise as though he were leaving it, but it would trail him a little more as the train bulleted toward his work, and he thought about when he and Gen fished in the streams and river along the mountain's edge or hiked on the trails lining the foothills.

After sealing its doors, the train accelerated from the station and, reaching a cruising speed, created the illusion of everything silent and noisy inside the car moving at a rate as ordinary as a flat line drawn across plain paper—familiar things moving regardless of sound or silence spiraling around them— but the outside blurred, save for the sun floating over the grassy horizon and near the jutting-up city. His day, for the first time, began with the sunrise and without his son.

. . .

By the time Mr. Matsumoto saw the sunrise, it was late afternoon of the previous day, in Milwaukee, and for Mr. Harrison, when he saw the sunrise, it reminded him what he had and no longer had as he prepared for his trip and long flight. He was tired but not tired looking. His face remained youthful enough to hide the last three months in ways exercise and alcohol were common remedies for people navigating similar stress and pushing through work projects. He ran on the treadmill at the gym paid for by the company—enough to break a sweat and reach a certain pulse before finishing with push-ups and air squats and a quick car-wash-like shower and cologne sprucing; he refused to avoid reality with drink the way his father had.

The younger Mr. Harrison had lost most of his hair by thirty-five, and the bald look, shaved by his hand, and his smooth face made him appear timeless and trustworthy, as though he neither aged nor was trapped in post-college immaturity—nor a desperate-enough forty-something executive grasping for a major deal that would transform his career and place him in his bosses' good graces. He spoke with an authority on business deals he had developed over his years with DynaRev; it was not a natural authority, which thundered in Dean Sr.'s voice, especially when amplified by alcohol, but it became his the more time and effort he put into it and the more subsidiaries the company accumulated during his tenure in the Mergers & Acquisitions department, of which his father, until retirement, had been a long-standing member whose presence the son had yet to emulate.

Mr. Harrison slid a fresh packet of trail mix into the front pouch of his computer bag, would buy a water bottle at the sundry store near his terminal, and stuffed one book in his carry-on. He had started the novel on a trip in March to Fargo where he coordinated the sale for a company manufacturing components for tractors and heavy machinery in the agriculture and mining industries; it was his last regional responsibility before taking on an overseas, international project. His wife suggested something "literary and deep" and not his usual collection of political thrillers or business articles. He wanted to read it because she enjoyed it, but the novel was too pretentious for him after he slogged through the first fifty pages: The book's back flap could have simply called the main character's job for what it was— sideshow circus worker—and not a metaphor reflecting her life.

With school lunches, his wife, and the upcoming trip on his mind, he had grabbed the book without thinking. He would come across it after the first stop in Chicago and upon crossing the flat lands of Kansas and its snow dumped atop brown grass wintry dry in spots that it was clipped into pockets of black dirt; he would bemoan his lack of being in the moment back at the house, as though the past stole from him whenever he welcomed it back in.

The airplane icon on the television screen in the headrest in front of him would show his location—barely out of the area he knew and represented for the company. It was mid-morning, Central Standard Time, when he left for the airport; it would be late night where he was headed—more than half a day ahead. He would leave the novel in his seat for someone else to take, after he had landed and changed planes at the international terminal.

But on his way to the Milwaukee airport, he had to drop off his kids at his sister's place. They liked Aunt Heather more than Aunt Laura (Mr. Harrison's wife's sister); neither child wanted to go. "Not too long, you guys. Aunt Heather and Uncle Todd can show movies you've been wanting to see. I'll be back before you know it." He looked at them over his shoulder as he drove and dodged putting them and the station wagon in a few accidents, which Annie, the seven-year-old, told him would happen were he to continue driving with one focus on Hunter and her and the other focus on his coffee and phone. From his position in the back seat, her five-year-old brother noted, "Mom doesn't do it that way," a reference to the lunch Hunter had peeked at—his fondness for the mustard to be on *one* side of bread, not both sides, of the ham sandwich, because too much mustard made the carrots taste funny—but Annie quickly corrected him with accounts, including all the times after Christmas something irritated their mother, who directed her anger at their father, the continuing source of her frustration, and as a result, lunch was fixed, packed in their backpacks, but not paired well.

After this clarification, the station wagon grew silent and chilled but was not as cold as the morning air and patches of snow languishing on lawns and sections of streets refrozen after spring warmth had loosened ice and broke through freezing temperatures for a momentary victory.

Mr. Harrison smiled at his kids, closed his phone, and idled in the left-turn lane while a silence finished scraping away everything else.

• • •

Snow topped the highest mountain points surrounding Kyoto, was neither thick nor cold enough to stick in the basin, and was fainter as spring crept up the rocky veins in varieties of greens. "A dusting…like freshly fallen ash," Mr. Matsumoto said, about which his family teased him, not at the inaccuracy of the description but at the poetry of it and his unwillingness to admit to his lyricisms while using them more as he aged.

He stepped off the train and made his way to the walkway leading from the station and toward the office—the sunrise following him like an orange balloon tied to his wrist by a long invisible string. As he turned northwest, toward the mountains, the distant bare snow brightened, and its emptiness may have been a symbol he intuited for starting over and for letting go of control of how things were or how he wanted them to be. But seeing mountaintop snow, he knew this blankness also covered whatever rested underneath; the spring warmth and the summer rain would dissolve it; and the immediacy of starting over may be a cycle of concealing and revealing.

He passed a section of the ward near his office and the public park where police found his son. At the station, the door to the inebriation holding cell opened. Mr. Matsumoto smelled liquor while standing in the hallway and waiting for his son to emerge. His clothes were wrinkled, as though stronger hands gripped him. One of the officers had forced Gen into the cruiser. The teen refused to be handled by the law and asked them if they knew who his father was—and if they didn't, they would be in for a sore awakening. He and the other teens he was with had finished bottles of liquor and threatened pedestrians, the report said, with "foul language and profane visuals." They held cans of spray-paint near large swaths of graffiti but claimed the cans belonged to vandals who were there before them.

Standing in front of the large glass panes composing his building's exterior, Mr. Matsumoto could not see anything inside. Figures behind him moved like washed-out navy-blue shadows, but they weren't people-shaped. His eyes were gray and soft in the glass. He stared at his small aquiline nose, which his son had inherited, and the long cheeks sinking in from all the length like tall sails losing wind. He noticed his hair—its silver-black strands draped over the top of his shirt collar, and he couldn't remember if he had grown it out as a memento for the day Gen would come home and they would reconcile; then he would cut it to its regular style parted down the middle, complimenting his widow's peak. He was sure his son would return, if only they could speak again to each other. He had met his son's close friend on a break Gen had from school. When Gen told him he and Yasuhito were more than friends, Mr. Matsumoto asked that be kept private for now—a family matter. The night he picked up his son from the police station Mr. Matsumoto yelled at Gen in a way he had never before—his anger focusing on the charges for public intoxication, the near-expulsion from classes due to poor grades, and the embarrassment and self-indulgence of these incidents, not on the two young men in love. The media circulated Gen's name and face but not because of his scholastic or athletic abilities as they had in the past.

In the minutes Mr. Matsumoto stood at his building's glass panes, no one from his staff checked on him; no one exited the revolving door and asked him if everything was all right; no one walked past him on the way to the office and disappeared into the revolving door, as he was about to do. He wondered if he had arrived earlier than usual. No. A holiday? No. Without having to consult his calendar, he was certain of these things. It was as though he was unaccounted for and not needed by anyone; as though he were a stranger lost in a city he was visiting for the first time; he had reached a point that could neither go further nor take him in where it had ended. Beyond the sun, snow, and mountains lay two certainties—the northern edge of the island and the Sea of Japan; water and land meeting sky. Mr. Matsumoto sighed at his reflection and watched a portion of the sun sliced off by a low section of the building. The sun was higher than when he walked here. Its yellow smudged on the windows, but neither the snow nor the mountains were visible any more. He turned around, made a phone call to his administrative assistant, and returned to the train station. He would not go into work today. He would try again tomorrow. He had to be here tomorrow.

• • •

Having spent his life in the upper Midwest, Mr. Harrison knew his share of snow, blizzards, and zero visibility. Ground snow unified everything underneath it into a smooth sheet, but elevated mounds were uncommon; the area's hills never grew into something larger than cold knuckles on a flat frozen hand. Mr. Harrison did not know mountains. He had seen them in media but never in person. He longed to snowboard in the Rockies, but he settled for cross-country skiing or driving a snowmobile over the Plains.

It was night when he left the United States and crossed the ocean. The sun was behind him, the moon shone over the wing, and he was losing time—a fourteen-hour jump into the future. The in-flight movie he faded in and out of watching had ended. Reading the novel he brought was pointless. Reading the magazines, while avoiding a piece of gum smashed between them and the airplane information card, was ineffective. He couldn't sleep, and when he tried, he couldn't calm himself. He opened his laptop and reviewed the contract and notes for the acquisition, but he could only think about his wife. He looked at the computer's calendar and the color-coded tags: FAMILY, WORK, PERSONAL. His kids had soccer games and a concert. The library needed volunteers for an Arts & Crafts Saturday Annie wanted to attend. Hunter needed new clothes. The station wagon's oil change was past due. His wedding anniversary had come and gone, and he and Leah did nothing for it during their silence—one thing they agreed on without having to speak.

Traveling west, past the West Coast, further than he had ever been, and crossing the time zones fabricated in the air and over the ocean would take away almost two days from him, propelling him into the future but not so far that he could distance himself from the present back home, as though this leapfrogged and illusory future could clarify an exact moment why his wife left—a point at which he could see everything behind him. His return flight, in a week, would replace the hours he had lost and would give him another illusion: starting over from the same spot he had vacated.

"Because I can, and because I want to," she had said to him, arms crossed while standing in the kitchen. The kids were asleep. He had wanted to talk, and these words were the only things she said. He pleaded for her to explain what she meant, to tell him what had broken down over the past year, which he thought was related to his time at work or her feeling of not being able to fulfill her career, having to put hers on hold while his accelerated. She admitted she wanted to be alone after not being alone for so long, having rushed into this life with him, everything around and connected to them having reached a mechanical torpor.

"And our family? Our friends?"

Leah didn't answer him. But before gathering some of her things, she said, "I want a break. It's not permanent."

In the cold mix of night and snow, red scarf sealing the top of her black wool coat, she left. The moon far from him, its effect closing around him as the minutes inside the airplane unspooled, matched the silence he heard as soon as he came home after work that night in January. There was no difference between one day ending and another waiting to begin.

Were he not given this M&A deal to oversee, Mr. Harrison would have requested to fly to Japan, taking a back-seat or behind-the-scenes role—anything to fly more than halfway across the world to suspend for a week his life back home, which he knew meant leaving his children during a confusing time, but he had no other option pausing his life's direction and momentum. He wanted this deal—to flesh out the offer after it was bandied as a rumor, sometimes as an inside joke for Marketing to generate interest in the company's stock, and to be the person who handled the names signed on the contract. His wife would say he was competing against the ghost of his father who was alive and intervened unseen. He would not say it that way, but he also wouldn't claim she was wrong.

In Tokyo, he looked for Mt. Fuji and was pleased to see half of it dipped in snow like a cookie covered in icing. Compared to the legends he heard about the Alps or the prowess of the Andes, the mountain was standalone vibrant. Early morning had begun back home, and his weather app showed slightly above-freezing temperatures and a small chance for flurries; the future-cast predicted typical spring-like weather for the greater Milwaukee metro area. Because of the time difference, he emailed his sister and told his kids hello and he missed and loved them. He gave them a countdown to when they would see each other again. He promised to talk to them as soon as he could; they could stay up late to do so.

While he sat in the terminal and waited for the regional jet to fly him to Osaka, he watched planes ascend into the fire-and-pink-charged sky; streams of air drifted off the wings like cotton pulled into strings and dyed in pastels. From there, a cab reserved by Matsumoto Engines would deliver him to his hotel in Kyoto in time for dinner and bed where he was neither hungry nor tired.

• • •

Everything aligned when they sat in the conference room. The morning dominated the windows as though bright colors had melted and an invisible force stretched them like glue for the clouds and the sheets of blue sky stuck there for the after-moment. And for the two businessmen in the room, with their computers, pens, cups of tea, and contract copies, the outside arrived shining on the chrome doorknobs, the bare walls, and the hardwood floor. The morning's alignment vivified the space, like lights signaling recollection for characters on a stage, and would not let them go. But the two men were not trapped. The doors to the conference room were not locked. The two men could not leave. They were obligated to stay.

In the middle of Paragraph 13.2, which discussed transference of intellectual property from Matsumoto Engines to DynaRev, Mr. Harrison paused and glanced toward the windows. The more he looked at the sunrise the more the colors lessened and the more the light, which lagged behind the colors in the room, like an echo trailing its source, neither broke apart the pain he held, as he had assumed large blocks of light would, and healing, not stowing, things in darkness, nor brightened everything with floodlights of vulnerability and confession. He noticed his colleague, sitting across but not directly from him, remained silent as he alternated between the contract and his laptop and drifted his attention from those things to the same space pulling in his. He thought his colleague was sophisticated, and he felt embarrassed when he wanted Mr. Matsumoto to quote haiku or a Zen insight into the human condition and suffering brought on by seeing things not as they are but how they are wished to be.

The two men made eye contact when they drifted from the job at hand to the windows, nodded at each other, and continued working through the contract, stopping to speak when a section required clarification, elaboration, or initials.

Mr. Matsumoto sipped from his tea, and when he did, he found the pour too cold and stood up, which caught the attention of Mr. Harrison, whose large eyes and soft face expressed he, too, could stand up and perhaps leave for more pressing matters. Mr. Matsumoto poured a glass of water and, before sitting, offered a glass to Mr. Harrison, who nodded and quietly said, "Thank you." The tall, lean man pivoted slightly in his chair, not to bring attention to himself or to slow the meeting but to see over his left shoulder where the American's eyes had been. He had not seen such an effect in some time—the role morning played in meaning—or if he had seen it, he had bypassed it as unconsciously as blinking. The sunrise swirled words inside him —words that could not change what happened between his son and him and words he wanted to say and could change the present before it slid too far away. He wondered if Mr. Harrison had ever been to a Packers game in the dead of winter. Mr. Matsumoto imagined wearing a large foam hat shaped and painted like a triangular block of cheese; he saw Gen wearing a hat, and the two of them would laugh in the bleachers and under a gray flurry-filled sky in the middle of the afternoon. Mr. Matsumoto did not prefer cheese—not that he was lactose intolerant, but having dairy sit in his stomach for a long time, slowly digesting, concerned him—but he would wear a cheese hat, and he would wear one with his son if he could leave this meeting, find his son, speak to him, correct imbalances, and fly to Mr. Harrison's point of origin. He did not see Mr. Harrison wearing such a hat. He did not think Mr. Harrison was much of a sports fan or an athlete at any point in his life. He looked like he would have remained a nobody at work had someone not intervened because this someone knew Mr. Harrison could not earn anything on his own. Mr. Matsumoto did not pity his colleague, but he did empathize. During the discussions, Mr. Harrison had handled all communications, directing them as much as he could. Mr. Matsumoto respected the initiative in the young man, but he questioned the cost. Yet, while the look-out-the-windows-look-away-when-caught continued, he could tell Mr. Harrison did not want to be here either; that the morning uncovered something inside Mr. Harrison, his paunchy face twitching over the contract and then outside, drew it out of him, and set it in the space between the sun, the snow-capped mountains, and him, where he could go were he not here.

Mr. Matsumoto wondered if this space—behind the building, shaped like a bowl, and in the middle of the morning's effect—was the same point he needed to reach; if what he and Mr. Harrison now had in common was neither the preservation of Mr. Matsumoto's great-great grandfather's company, albeit by a multi-national, foreign-based company acquiring it, nor Mr. Matsumoto assuming, by completing this deal, Mr. Harrison would earn respect in the eyes of the board and people closest to him, perhaps employed for a little longer, one pressure taken off, new pressures tightened, but there was no other place to go but into the tenor of things, and it was a halfway point between the two men, like climbers scaling opposite sides of a mountain rising

above the clouds, everyone at the bottom asking where they had

disappeared, and into the fog circling the peaks, the twin engines

of memory and pain pushing them to the top, where once scaled,

isn't what it was believed to be from the ground, attained too late,

the pursuit of ascent evaporating, and now evening coming on.

Rail Time

This train starts again, starts making its way from the coast and back to the station, where we started before reaching the sea and the cliff-side town wrapped in a gray refusing to relent as the sun hits midday somewhere behind the clouds. We slid here, emerged from the valley and the woods, and met the sea as though our descent would continue across asphalt streets, sand and kelp, and finally water—this train pulled to the sea; this train now pulling us back up as the sharp turn comes again until the shoreline bends at its eroded elbow and the ocean mottles behind us, the coast disappearing into harder land unchanged by waves and chunks of the earth's floor exposed at low tides. One whistle pipes before we are isolated; after that, no whistle, because there is nothing and no one to inform we are on the way before they or us could block the way. *Among here*—the motion repeats its verse as this train chugs along. The singsong motion takes us further into the mountains, toward their striated edge, and cuts its way across a sequence of events not yet gone cold, like a ghost asking about its body.

We enter the point where we had been many minutes ago, when we were on our way to the ocean and its waves and where we noticed the air had changed from effervescent to heavy with salt, the light surrendering to the coast, and we knew we were close to the halfway point before we would turn around. And now at this same point, but facing the other way, beyond it, up ahead, our bodies closest to the open window of our car, we see them in the distance—the stretch of wildflowers. They will thicken the closer we get, specks of colors filling in, piece by piece, tufting up from the ground until they overflow the valley; will start wrapping tree trunks, climbing over fences and alongside streams running stronger because of melted mountain snow, new contours carved or old courses expanded by winter storms. We will pass them again—those flowers we saw on our way from the station—and when we see them, we will realize how close this train is to stopping, how much farther it has returned to the station where our other car waits, where life will snap back into a larger and more complicated present.

What did I miss the first time through? Of seeing what we passed on the way out passing us on the way in? Landscape in spectra reverse; fingers thumping across palm-muted strings as the wheels and the engine sound off. Say them—these flowers soon surrounding the car's windows. You know them better than I know them; you said their names on our way here. Say them while we still have time because the signs of a previous time are coming, the past revisited as the present becoming past as soon as we pass through it, where we had been and will find ourselves again.

Slowly the late afternoon light appears and opens the day as wide as a parting sea someone could take you through; this train does. The wind has died down. The air is newborn. There are ferns the size of a giant's hands. The big trees and the evergreen mountain ridges cool the sunlight. The ocean, with its simplicity, reaching it and on our way to it, pulled away so much pressing on us—how we changed above, at, and now back above sea level—the horizon scrubbed free of the ocean, where the stars will be.

Grays dissipating into patchwork greens and a blue sky; the soft ground toughening under the weight of the mountain range; redwoods breaking the salt-charged air; other trees fanning out, not flattened or worn down by shore wind; large trunks upright: It is spring, and we can't be inside ourselves; we said today seemed like a good day *to be* rather than *to seem.*

Ascending a slope, this train moves slower than it moved on the way through here the first time, and we accept we will arrive slower than we want; the present can fend off the past for a little more; the return must end better than the start, until, yes, we come full circle. All these points along the way, moments retelling moments, connecting them like a string through pages: They are still there; we will be, too. Say them.

Once this train hits cruising speed, people aboard move about the cars, and if we move about, the conductor reminds us, step *Yellow to yellow*, caution line to caution line, minding the gap between cars, ground-time rushing under us. When we started, before the ocean, before here, we sat quietly and watched the landscape roll by; watched the red-gray rails ahead of us, the station behind us. And now returning, we want to say hello to everyone who walks past us, maybe because we are on our way back; maybe because the guitarist aboard this train sings songs of an American spirit wondering where it had been and where it could fit in; and maybe because this is a way to say there are seasons in which so many stones are thrown until there is no shelter from them; and there are seasons in which to build a shelter with those same stones while the rest of us in the streets go about unnoticed or ignored, our heads down, not out of fear or ignorance but attending to something incapable of words the first or second time—or a lifetime.

Desire has a sound. This train's clicks and clacks matter for the moment. The heart expands to take in as much as the eyes. We've been trying for years to be less planned; to be more surprised by what rises in the garden each spring after throwing seeds here and there—a new sequence of colors is better because it's different at first glance, and yet we know it's the same result in a different light. If you could make a song about this, you would have to include water finding its way to the roots and shoots of small bright things outside windows, including where we sit as this train dips before recovering its upward move.

The moment sits upon our tongues—what will be this memory looping until it hardens like a pearl. We look out the window. Here it was, and now here it is—the first full field soon passing. Say them to me, to the two of us—these words, their names, this secret waving between us, no one else to tell as we are not alone: kids trying to grasp at many things floating by; other passengers moving from car to car to get better views or to hang out open windows; songs about a country, landscapes, and people within; the scenery passing, time coming around, this train chugging at a speed slower than what the years take away.

Tunnel ahead—the halfway point soon to be reached. Across from us on the map hanging near what would have been the coat rack decades ago, the route like black paint dripped across canvas: one square at the station; the other square near the sea. There is no turnaround this way back in—but an extension of cutting straight through; of adjusting speed through changes in the terrain; of counterbalance. Time here shortens, and colors flank this train. Say them as though the light on the other side of the tunnel will never reach us, but if it does, saying them would continue not a singular, vague past but two vivid, equally yoked presents carrying us—the land stretching from forests to waters and back again.

Letting go of feeling half-alive, we reached a point where we knew we no longer waited; the previous parts of our lives in which we saw ourselves floating, as though we were trapped in a terminal flooded with anxiety, neither waiting nor anticipation but searching for recess. And when we came across the wildflowers the first time, it was as though I found a tendril far away from its parent, and you, saying its name and those of the others blooming nearby, pulled all of them, brought them into our midst like a sailor pulling a deep anchor, until the pulling on our end became a pulling from the other end—the source pulling us closer because it was firm in the ground. And once we reached it, I realized how beautiful and rare they were—beautiful because they were rare—and I had no knowledge of them, no words for them. You knew the names for all of them and said they were common in these parts, but what made them rare was their space made possible by the winter precipitation uncommon in years, this coverage we are seeing once again.

This train, it seems, is the only thing on our side—these few bright things serve the many. And we are close to entering the tunnel. On the other side: a return to a different time. Say them. It will grow dark and cold, and when we are through, there will be only so many miles left to say something about these things outside our window; these things with us now will be the soft tissue coloring the skeleton of memory. Say them as though we could stay because the things we can say are the things taking shape and have become possible because of the limits of who we are.

To not be alone; to be in this world but not of it; to not be fixed: It has taken a straight line bent into a roundabout to realize this; to realize we barely recognize ourselves—it takes a spring palette and a clean light to see what we are; and to realize this day is now part of us, inseparable, ours, arriving somehow in the nick of time when a twilight was ready to cover what we have or could lose. But tomorrow could be a different lens through which we see: Today's headlines will be waiting for us—speculations of avalanches growing from the sight of a few fallen rocks. These colors couldn't be anywhere else but under and around this train. The fields are heavy with pools of paint.

Daylight again: The countdown tumbles as we exit the tunnel. We know few spots remain. Say them. Scattershot neighborhoods and timber mills: A few remaining in operation flicker pass; the rest are ruins and survive as images filtered and delivered to other parts of the world. It is Sunday. No one works at the mills today; there are cars and trucks, but they are quiet. Wildflowers bloom under the busted window frames, inside the dockyards, and alongside rusted racks large enough to hold logs. Emerging from their houses or standing in open doors or sitting in cars at the rail crossing, people wave at us. Children wave. The elderly wave. From our car, we wave on our way in as we waved on our way out. This simple, natural gesture: people waving at each other as they roll by; as though waving holds words enough to express one of compassion's roots; as though waving from far away is best for someone whom you can never know and can never reach.

And we don't want to stop and reverse; this train has done that. But we want time to fall away before coming back—not in full costume, as it was when it left—but with open hands in which only so much can be held because there would be less to let go. We know this train can't keep time or the outside world from us. We know the world twists and turns with us; stays put regardless of where we are or where we place ourselves within because we are without, often momentarily. And we know the return can't transform us in such a short time—the station at the end and the waiting world—yet we wonder if we will change, what has changed within us or possibly could change after this, and if it is brief and won't stick without more time. Or maybe there is no change; maybe we return as when we started and this continuity is more important than this pause of time, this get-away from what we know or don't openly talk about, such as these people waving or the entropy we carry within us, this bound-to-end, which doesn't necessitate sadness but should remind us why hope strips away films deposited on time until what is seen through the other end is neither a light nor a darkness but a place proving one song wrong: In the end, it's neither a love you make nor a love you take but a love available and never-ending; in the end there was more than you and I.

Sunshine flits through the trees. This train parallels the road snaking its way from here, through the mountains, and finally reaches the town nestled miles from the Pacific. Cars and trucks take it; the locals take it at a more confident speed than the tourists. *In time*—this phrase taking us elsewhere where we wait in the shadow of the car's roof. Once we are here, deeper in the valley, it is now complete: The light has all but finished its oceanic shift—fully inland and subject to evergreens and deciduous spaces and the shapes of the town and the people who have stopped waving and return to what they were doing before we passed through—a private past made present, and private, again.

Signs and mileage for the town close in, as do billboards and advertisements for places to eat and rest: historic buildings, franchises, a charming downtown. A camera icon tells us the next scenic route waits further up the interstate, nearly straight north —the same county enveloping so many small towns that its two gateways are *Sequoia sempervirens* and waves building and breaking up the coastline until centuries of observations fortify the changes. Streetlights multiply. A red squiggle in the green valley, we are over the final ridge—the scenery the same as it was on this train's descent toward the water—and we joke that going back downhill is akin to a classic movie's black-and-white car fixed in front of a screen rolling out the same black-and-white scenes and the illusion of everyone inside moving while staying put. The last trestle before the station squeaks under the brakes, the wheels, and us. The land has leveled; it cannot drop or rise anymore. Around this train, the small flames of wildflowers remain. Up ahead, all this must end. Say them.

As it blurred everything behind us like salt water in eyes looking for the shore, we jumped ahead of time; now we have jumped back into time as it reframes us. The world will wrap around us once we step off this train. There will be news and new data and rumors and rumors of rumors; the previous day's story will change; someone will add to or subtract from a story running on opinions and promising quick solutions to old concerns. Gray skies may become grayer before a cloudless blue cycles back. And we may not realize this for days—or ever—and if we do, it may be too late in one sense but not a conclusion in another. Seasons will roll on by, and the windows, such as the ones we find ourselves looking out of from this train, our heads nearly out the windows like dogs in good weather, will capture them and will be the point where you can feel buoyant when the next week lines up with a new chorus of concerns, which happens more than once in a lifetime and often comes on so robust it blots out blemishes and beauty marks distinguishing one day from the next. But other moments will arrive with multiple sediments brought in from various points along their journeys: sand, shells, seeds, feathers, bones; tiny particulates uncovered during a walk or on the cusp of waking from a dream with a door opening to an upper room and music therein—a feast with those you know, who know you as intimately as sunshine floating on water, and who want you to see the burning filament that is the horizon every morning and evening.

Soon the station will look like an Old West movie set well past its prime. The tracks have brought us near the mechanics' pit where shells of iron horses stand. This train can't keep going. Wildflowers taper off. Something must be said of them because there is no escaping them. Last whistle before this train pulls into the station and cuts its engine and we have to return to what we momentarily left behind. Say them as we pass and because we can never take them with us—they would fall apart if we did. They are already named, but say them: these purples, yellows, whites, oranges, and greens among us, seen in open spaces and shadows; these things clearing out one quiet section from the rest of the world. Fiddlehead, tickweed, tidy tips, hillside daisy, lupine, poppies, wild mustard. That it took going out and then coming back in to be reminded why.

Nothing Slowing Down or Stopping In Between

The horse appeared mid-sentence, which Carmen could not mention while on the phone with her colleagues. Heavy breath warmed her neck and shoulder while she discussed handling a client's portfolio and its underperforming assets. Hoping the humid draft would dissipate, the junior exec tugged at her shirt collar as her computer screen reflected the backlit horse head. She snapped around after she was asked to confirm a company had "enough in its legs to carry itself to the fiscal year's finish line."

The lanky blonde rubbed her eyes. Hours had passed since she returned from a noodle-heavy lunch, and she wondered if carb-fog had settled across her brain's byways—a fog so thick that a late-afternoon espresso could not cut through. But how did a 1,200-pound animal slip by security and cameras? Did he waltz into Dean & Assoc. as though he had an appointment? Ms. Zee, your four-fifteen is here, and he's a horse. Her office's only door was closed; the two locks worked. Were the other floors and her coworkers literally and metaphorically out to lunch? Had they vacated early for the holiday? A prank, she guessed, from the emotionally underdeveloped thirty-four-year-old business manager and maybe some of his immediate colleagues. They had enough clout with upper management to haze the new junior executives and handed out asinine errands to the unpaid summer interns during their first weeks on the job, such as combing archives for deceased clients who coincidentally shared a first, middle, and last name with notorious living inmates, having them call the prison, and set up a time for an annual review. But this?

The horse threw its head and flapped its lips. Stress, Carmen diagnosed and chased aspirin with half an energy drink diluted with water. She quickly typed her end-of-day tasks and reviewed last week's productivity meetings until the horse, clomping its large hoofs, stood next to her. He was not there two and a half hours ago when she left for lunch because she had glanced at the space where her indoor plant had not survived winter—and where sunshine, dust, and dead bug shells littered the corner before the horse dominated the space on the eve of her and her sisters' birthday. Sleek, reddish-brown, soot-streaked legs, black-tipped ears, black whip of a tail: He had all the markings of a classic bay—a thoroughbred. Grey hairs sprinkled along his frame and muzzle. And he looked familiar to her.

"Going to reach out to your sisters?" he asked.

She was indeed going to, and the horse looming over her in her office concerned her less than his mindreading. Receiving a text from Carmen or not, her sisters would perceive something awry; they filled in premonitions the more they concentrated on their appearances, like children staring at clouds. The fraternal triplets had shared this connection since they were young— invisible wires burning hot when charged.

"You should. They should be here, too," he continued. "They're part of this."

"This *what*? How did you get in?"

He threw his soft gray-pink nose at the door. "Don't you remember me?"

She wanted to say yes but leaned back in her chair and crossed her arms. "No."

"But you do. You and your sisters' birthday twenty-two years ago."

Carmen knew exactly what he referenced; the memory rose its neck out of long-ago waters long gone dark.

"You and the other two didn't do such a hot job of taking care of me. You girls came home that one day, and I was gone."

"What does this have to do with me?"

"Not just you. Your sisters, too." His heavy belly shivered. "I did go to another farm, and life there was OK. They found out my sire and his dad were both decent racehorses, nothing like being in one of the Triple Crown races or anything one notch beneath that. More like the minor leagues of horseracing. Very minor. But they got the job done. Mom did, too. She had a long line of family members that raked in the money in Ireland. That lit up their eyes. So, they started training me. And the odds were smaller that I could ramp up being a racehorse, but those odds seemed pretty good, given my background."

"So you became a racehorse."

"But not by my own hand, so to speak. I wasn't amazing. You can see my stats online." He threw his blocky head at Carmen's computer. "Equine Stat dot com. I had a different name when I was with you. When I raced, I was known as Cleo's Love."

Carmen typed in the site's database. After clicking the little shaded-in horse-in-full-stride icon for the Search button, the history of his appearances filtered under his name. Carmen covered her mouth after bursting out laughing. "You were awful."

"Hey, come on." He blinked his big dark eyes at her response; his thick neck bobbed. "OK, so, yes, I didn't exactly 'crush it' in my years as a full-miler."

"Or as a three-quarter runner. Not even close."

"They thought maybe I could hack it with fewer furlongs to gas out. When it rained, I had issues with wet turf. Plus, my stomach did not like the diuretics."

"Your average position was seventh? *Seventh?* The handicap comments say 'Bellies up too early but pretty typical,' 'His chevron silk was the best thing about him,' 'Is faster taking a bathroom break than running.'"

The horse rustled about, his hooves clicking on the hardwood floor, his ears pulsing back. "Anyway, this is where we are…you and I and your sisters. You and your sisters owe me."

"No. This has gone on too far." She glanced out her office window. *Did I get hit by one of those male-feminist baristas and didn't know it? Maybe he blinded me with his pink hat and I'M STILL WITH HER t-shirt before clocking me.*

"You're very much alive," the horse replied out loud to her thoughts.

Carmen glared at the bay raising and lowering his feet as though they moved on a treadmill. "What do you want from us?"

"I want to ride in the city. You and Melanie and Lana could not hack it enough to take care of me. That's all I want. A ride in the city."

Carmen looked at the horse when he said her sisters' names; she had been thinking of them and the brief time they had with the horse in their lives and how he now stood next to her. "We were eight."

"You didn't take care of the horse that was your birthday gift."

"We messed up. Can't we call it like that and off you go?"

The horse's tail thrashed the air. "I am the one paying for your domino effect."

Carmen glanced at her cell phone. It was late in the afternoon. No one would be checking on her because she was a junior exec, no longer a lackey at the bottom of the company's hierarchy who needed to check in with managers above her; she could come and go as she pleased as long as the work got done, which, given her position, corner office, bonus package, stock options, and lack of micro-managing from her superiors, she did —under budget and under deadline. And it was Memorial Day weekend; the offices were empty by now. "Why the city?"

"How many times have you seen a horse out and about enjoying the city?"

"Other than parades or police horses?"

"They aren't enjoying themselves. I have cousins on the force. They are working. I want to ride around the city. I have never been up and down the main streets. I'm an old horse, on the way out."

"OK. You're in town now, so…" Carmen picked up her cell phone and fired off texts, which, before she did, the horse looked down at the blue message-bubbles from her sisters and then directly at her.

Soon after, the office door creaked open, and wrapping their fingers and eyes around the door's edge, the two sisters crept in like burglars, and once inside, they stood dumbfounded before the horse lowering his chin over Carmen's shoulder. Confirming Carmen was safe relieved the sisters, but she was unnerved, and they had suspected as much, knowing her messages weren't the results of late-afternoon drinking, career advancement, or upper-management shenanigans.

"Mr. Bojangles Brownie Jazz Hands!" Lana screamed. "You came back like I knew you would!"

The horse looked at Carmen with a *See, told you* look on his face.

The junior exec stood up, dusted white whiskers from her black slacks, and walked over to her sisters. "Did you bring the van?"

Melanie could not stop staring. "Is he…?"

"Yeah."

"How do we…?

After the three sisters accepted the horse was real and what they saw in front of them and what he asked of them was no dream or prank to be uploaded onto a website, they debated how to move him—a debate volleyed back and forth under composed emotion until arguments heated, punctuated by the sisters' standard high-pitched vocal tones: Carmen, as first born, having pounced on the lead and her my-way-or-the-highway opinion; Melanie as the middle sister left to defend her own ideas or to be coerced under Carmen's tight-clawed reign; and Lana the baby, who, after Carmen had shoved aside Melanie in the womb to arrive first, was born breech but showed no ill effects of such position once she entered the world near midnight—her tiny butt straddling, the family noted, often with a laugh, two different days, right down the middle ("At the crack of dawn," their dad joked), and willing to agree with either of her sisters, depending on which one was winning the argument, either by evidence or by vocal intensity. The horse intervened and suggested the device that helped him reach the office, and when he suggested the elevator, the fraternal triplets blankly looked at each other and realized he was correct with his obvious suggestion and that a horse standing in an office in the heart of the city had suggested it.

• • •

The elevator to the parking garage dinged open. Industrial-sized motors hummed in the vents lining the walls and ceiling. The three sisters and the horse walked to the van with its paint scheme of an Americana schoolhouse (red brick, steeple, golden bell) and books scattered about, labeled MATH, FOREIGN LANGUAGE, ENGLISH, and SCIENCE on the spines. Parked under flood lamps buzzing overhead, the van was the sole remaining vehicle.

"Who's the teacher?" the horse asked, stopping in front of bold-letters.

TUTORS ON WHEELS
K–12 MOBILE TUTORING THAT COMES TO YOU!

"Teach-*ers*," Melanie emphasized, thumbing to Lana and herself. "She handles Spanish and the basics of grade school, while I handle high schoolers and seniors who are headed to college or community college."

"None of you ever seemed to be caregivers. Well, shall we?" The horse clicked his teeth into a big smile, as much as he could, given some decay, and retuned his attention to the side door slid open by Lana who rode shotgun with one earbud in, one earbud dangling.

Melanie helmed the wheel and started the van. The horse and Carmen shared space in the back equivalent to a stuffed clown car. Having learned over the years that accessories on hand was much easier than loading and unloading them on a daily or weekly basis, the younger sisters kept gear inside the van: portable desks; a whiteboard; the innards of what was to be a smart-board installed sometime in the near future; and wires, connectors, lights, and dry-erase markers.

All three lived together in a decent-sized house in one of the better city neighborhoods. Carmen's bonus from earlier in the year helped with the down payment, but Melanie, at four months pregnant, waffled about moving out or having Baby Daddy move in, which Carmen had been vocal about—and not in a positive way. After graduating from college and spending some time "finding herself," mainly among train routes running along mountain resort towns bordering France and Switzerland, Lana was merely excited to be with her sisters once again and knew being older was a better time for them to live together than when they were younger and more prone to dramatic outbursts, which reemerged when the three occupied the same space.

As the van approached the gate, Melanie stopped and asked Carmen for her parking-garage card because she didn't want to pay for the time spent in the space, and she shouldn't have to pay because she needed all the money she had for Baby May, whose name reflected the current month until Melanie and Baby Daddy agreed to an official name, and, Melanie pointed out, it was Carmen who requested them and the van, making it sound like the *Titanic* had smashed into the granite-and-glass iceberg that was her corner office and all hope was sinking with an on-board horse their parents had given to them and then took away when they were eight—*and*, the middle child continued, because she and Lana had to leave their own work, which is a career Carmen has never respected, it would only be fair for Carmen to use her parking pass and not have the least-profitable sister pay for parking and have Baby May experience trauma and drama.

Melanie didn't say as much, but the middle sister's litany bubbled under the surface of her "Should we pay for parking, or is there another way?" To which Carmen knew the tactic her middle sister played, having anticipating it while reading her body language seconds before the question arrived and, dropping her head to the right, grimaced and asked Lana if Melanie would be willing to say what she wanted to say and not beat around the bush, as she typically did. Lana looked up from her phone and its refreshed stream of social-media content and offered a non-confirming "Sure." To which Melanie defended her position and said, "Never mind, Carmen. I'll take care of it *again*. I can't see why we can't use your pass. It's OK, Baby May." She rubbed her belly and coasted the van onto the crowded street wedged between lineups of tall buildings.

"Because I didn't come to work in my car today," Carmen responded. "I took the metro, and the card will only work if you enter with it. They know if you're sharing a card with someone who didn't enter."

"Lana, tell her we're not stealing anything."

"Hey, Carmen, we're not…"

"Mel."

"Ladies," the horse intervened, farting; the fetid smell congested the van.

Looking at each other, the sisters noted he didn't apologize yet asked them to remain focused on the task at hand: driving him around the city. Melanie and Lana rolled their eyes and rolled down their windows.

"This is the Financial District," Carmen spoke through her sleeve covering the bottom half of her face. "We'll pass some major brokerage houses and some of the biggest banks in the country."

The horse looked the grand buildings up and down, most of them reflecting the red-orange sunset and the amount of cars, trucks, and pedestrians choking the streets.

"We're headed north. Once we cross Fifteenth is when you'll notice businesses change."

"They'll become more commercial and consumer focused. Clothes, jewelry, accessories, that kind of stuff."

The horse nodded at each sister's contribution and kept his milky eyes glued to the various storefronts and people passing beside the van's tinted windows.

After flipping off a motorcyclist who nearly scraped the sliding door, Melanie soothed her belly, glanced in the rearview mirror, and said, "If you don't me asking, what's this all about? Carmen made it sound like the end of the world and that we're all to blame. Is she the one to blame?" The middle child's brown eyes swiveled to the back seat but were met with no response from the arctic blonde who had, Melanie surmised, heard but deliberately ignored her.

"Well, as I was saying earlier to Carmen, we all have a history together. You girls dropped the ball on me."

"I don't think we can be responsible for that at all. Do you?"

He looked straight at Melanie. "Very much so."

At that point, inside the horse's deep, resonant accusatory response, a confederacy formed between the back seat's human occupant and the van's driver. Melanie and Carmen glared at each other but not out of spite for the other one; they had found a moment in which sprouted a single thought liberating and uniting them.

As Carmen cleared her throat and mentioned some of the diverse foods along Food Truck Row, Melanie shifted in her seat and, the top half of her belly catching the bottom half of the steering wheel, changed lanes, heading away from the Financial District and toward the tangles of on-ramps and off-ramps.

"Mr. B?"

"Yes, Lana?"

"I want you to know I tried hard to make it all work out with you back in the day."

"Oh, Lana!" Carmen and Melanie protested. "You were as bad as us."

"I did a lot, y'all!"

"You barely touched anything. The food, the grooming, the cleaning up was all Melanie and me."

"All you wanted to do was treat him like some kind of magical unicorn."

"They're right."

Curling brown hair around her fingers and switching podcasts, the baby sister shrugged at the horse's confirmation.

"You kept putting a cardboard horn under my halter," he continued. "And you sprinkled glitter all over me. That didn't help me or my situation much. You're as much at fault as the other two. Your sisters complained about the chores, but at least that meant they knew about the chores. You *only* wanted to play with me, and when you were done, you were done."

Lana frowned and pretended to ignore the horse's allegations, but his accusations betrayed and shocked her. Anything reminiscent of childhood innocence started to bend under the weight of a fact she knew was not moot. "Let's get out of here," she mumbled, a string of words only her sisters heard.

As soon as Lana mentioned a change of scenery, Carmen and Melanie knew a piece had tilted into place—the two older sisters having picked up on the mood change in their baby sister, both earbuds now jammed into her ears, the podcast's higher volume leaking, the van's temperature frosting over, the air becoming heavier with brooding and a grinding silence, save for the single thought passed between each sister, who amended it to her own personality and level of perceived blame and determining what should be the next step, a thought so communicable that it rolled the youngest sister like a handful of mud slapped onto a growing and unstoppable landslide, under the growing mass of the confederacy established minutes ago between the two older sisters who were first and second to detest how their thirtieth birthday was unfolding, joined now by the final sister to arrive.

The van slowed in front of a sign for tourism showing the Historic Waterfront to the right, shopping to the south, and up on the left, the Museum District. Traffic tightened around them. They told the horse the city had played a trick on them and they had been hopeful of moving about the main thoroughfares and auxiliary streets with ease, as the horse had asked, but as Carmen pointed toward the bug-guts-and-bird-poop-splattered window, it was not meant to be—an effect of so many things wanting to be outside with its fire-charged sky and scraps of clouds not yet assembled into gray blocks but looking like they could at any time and change expectations and the course of events. They would have to find another way to clear the differences between the four of them.

"Let's go to the big park outside of town."

"Good idea, Lana."

"Aren't there trails out there?" he asked.

"It's more open and quiet," all three chimed.

• • •

It was late in the day, after sunset, when the van stopped inside the regional park. The horse tossed his nose toward the door handle and commented again on the state of things between the sisters and him. Carmen opened the door and

95

stepped out to give him plenty of space; Melanie and Lana stared at the sky's orange dissolving into blue-black. The horse was hesitant and slow—perhaps due to his age and health; perhaps, the sisters wondered, due to a burden weighing on him, not depression but realizing this day's ending wasn't matching his expectation and he had neither weighed returning to the sisters' lives nor considered their reactions or their semblance of control and refusal after his reappearance. He started walking toward the trails winding around the edges of cliffs falling into a deep ravine where a river rushed at the bottom.

"While we waited for you two to show up," Carmen said as the horse opened up his stride on the trail, "he told me, 'They put AVAILABLE next to my name every time the day's race card was printed. Do you know what that means?' I said, 'No,' 'It means I'm on display, regardless how I run in that race. It means *Make an offer…* I'm *For Sale*. I was sold to the highest bidder.'"

"Lots of horses change hands. It's more common than he made it out." Lana held up her phone glowing with the results of her rapid real-time search.

The sisters agreed they were tired of the horse; of being blamed for his lot in life when they did not have developed-enough minds and character; how he tried to make them feel guilty because of their lack of foresight at age eight; how they had abandoned him when they were young and were responsible for his existence and well-being and they had completely changed the direction of his life of which this day was the final fragment. Sitting in city traffic, he hammered on about the horrible of stewards they had been, forcing him to be a racehorse when he wasn't supposed to be a racehorse—and one so bad other owners, trainers, jockeys, and race fans joked that betting on him was a faster and easier way to lose handfuls of money than going through a divorce or having a legitimate criminal rob them at gunpoint.

"What are we going to do?"

"We should let him be. He'll go away."

"He'll follow us around. He found us today. He could find us again."

They remembered their parents had said that life's lemons can be turned into lemonade and sour moments—such as no longer having a horse for a birthday gift; such as realizing the amount of work, effort, and discipline responsibility requires—was an opportunity to reflect on two important lessons life handed out: Surprises—good and bad—are surprises for a reason; and not everyone in this world lives a fortunate life, to which their parents added being thankful for what was at hand mattered more than what was missing.

The fraternal triplets watched the horse gallop before stopping and catching his breath near a fence line with handrails rotted away into the dark air, beyond which lay the ravine and, inside, the river.

"I think they needed the money."

"You think Mom and Dad sold him for money? For themselves?"

"They've never said why, other than lectures about being accountable."

"We've never asked why."

"Why start now?"

The three sisters agreed the horse had become a nuisance. They wondered who was more of an albatross—he or they? They laid out their options, including the single thought formed under their unified alliance.

"We can't do that. Can we?"

"He said he was 'on the way out.'"

"Would that put us out of *our* misery?"

"Whatever you want to do."

They watched the horse buckle a little in the grass—perhaps his old hooves hitting a rock or a divot; perhaps his knees giving out—and they knew a horse's existence was saturated in an awareness of surroundings. A horse had an innate trepidation of being prey and never being a predator. No natural defenses were built into a horse's body, save for a large-engine heart and musculature propelling itself from the predator.

"Do you still want to go to Tucci's tonight?"

"We can't miss our birthday tiramisu."

"We *won't* miss it."

"It's a tradition now."

"Plus, it's a Big One."

"One of *the* Big Ones."

"Don't forget the other Big Ones. Ear-piercing at twelve, first year as a teenager, Sweet Sixteen, adulthood, and legal drinking age."

"Did Quarter-Life-Crisis Twenty-Five count?"

"It should."

"With us it should."

The horse wandered around the park; he seemed stunted or lost in the coming dark. The sisters moved away from the van, walked over to him, and they asked if he remembered the creek that, when they were eight, divided the World of Rainbows and Talking Stuffed Animal Teatime from the Hungry Gold Dragon living on the other side of the creek where, back then, there was nothing but dark woods that over time, they had seen and heard, had transformed into high-end homes for the burgeoning tech community moving out of the city for cheaper costs of living and "that country air." Yes, the horse remembered, and they asked him if he would like to see it up close. Yes, he said, and added he did not like to swim unless he was fleeing something. He asked if this was that place with the creek because he thought he was at a park and came here in a van, not on foot, but this, he noted, did not explain his burning joints because that usually happened when he walked too much. His ears flapped like birds leaving trees; he seemed confused. Yes, the sisters nodded their heads.

The night had cooled until it felt like anything could happen with regards to the power of the air. On the way to the creek, there was talk of flowers popping from the ground.

As they got close to the missing fence line, the sisters knew it would take all of them to push him, scaring him in the process. The above-seasonal-average snow in the mountains had melted and rapidly increased the river's flow. The horse noticed the water's speed and some of the rocks below whitewashed by the quickly moving waves; he didn't want to go any further, but the sisters told him not to worry and called him closer to the edge of the trail, where the dirt sloped and turned into slippery, irregular rocks where fence posts used to be.

And then rain fell. The sisters tried sending a message to each other, a message involving the image of a light flashing from red to green, with nothing slowing down or stopping in between, but the clouds and the rain blocked delivery and reception, the message flying on one wing in the many shadows in the air between them, the weather and its double-edged sword of ruining a moment while simultaneously offering another moment that quickly lags behind, like a balloon tied to a wrist pulling it through a breeze, the climate coming to the rescue at the last minute, as it sometimes does.

A Fine Day Will Burn Through

Moynihan Dairy lay on the outskirts and was a typical-looking modern farm: ribbons of gravel winding inside squared-off pastures and stretches of tall-grass fields; a pond; two silos—one rusted and the other painted green with the dairy's name and shamrocks emblazoned on the cone; skeletal outbuildings; hay bales and seed sacks; two delivery vans; hoses and tubes; industrial-sized equipment; barns, including a long one dominating the middle of the land; a main house circled by trucks and SUVs; and thick metal fences demarcating MD from surrounding farms and ranches.

The foothills crested in the distance, the Saturday afternoon sun deepening blacks and blues of the Rocky Mountains and highlighting patches of snow. Weeks ago, during his research, Josh saw a drone photo of the dairy provided by Boulder Area Animal Activists. The photo and writer cast the farm as seeping with horror and continuous disregard for food regulations and depicted the farm's logo of a jovial cow with an Irish-style derby snug between its horns as the overlord of a nightmare company spreading pesticide-laden dairy products and dismantling human genetic sequences.

But the mistreated-animals-poisoned-consumers fantasy fogging Josh's head broke up as his dad's champagne-colored station wagon turned off Mill Pass Road and onto Happy Cows Lane, low-hanging branches scraping the doors and bumpers, and rattled under the welcome sign flanked by two large green shamrocks and inscribed with WELCOME TO MOYNIHAN DAIRY – CREAMY GOODNESS SINCE 1905.

"Looks like you're going in a boy and coming out a man," Reggie whispered to Josh, punching him repeatedly in the arm and evolving his gestures of faux milking into embracing an imaginary bovine.

Josh ignored his older brother and his baseball-calloused hands moving up and down imaginary teats.

"Bestiality's still a sin, right, Dad?"

"Reggie!" Mr. de Luca shouted, glaring into the rearview mirror and at the teenage face gaggling in the back seat. "What did I say about those jokes?"

Mrs. de Luca spun in her seat, the aroma of lavender wafting from under her dark curls and off her delicate shoulders, and smiled at Josh. "What time, Mr. Actor?" she asked, upbeat.

Her smooth, unblemished face in the afternoon light repulsed Josh. "What?"

"To pick you up. You can't be here *all* day." She flashed her eyes and high cheekbones at him. "We have errands, and Reggie wants the car to go to the movies with Tabitha."

"He said they close at five on the weekends."

Mrs. de Luca glanced at Mr. de Luca. "How about three? That's two hours. You can only research so much, right? You have to make it all come alive on stage."

Josh frowned and pulled his head to the road as the car turned into a flat space between the main barn, house, and a massive metal gate. A tractor rumbled a few yards from them; a collie, bouncing through the grass, sprung close to the big tires, adding a few barks. The station wagon rocked to a stop and idled. "That's fine, Janis."

Mrs. de Luca sniffled as she faced the blue sky framed in her window.

"*Josh,*" his father scolded before softening his voice. "What we talked about."

"Love you, *Mom.*"

"Not now, Reggie."

"Three is fine." Josh thrust one leg out the door. His bright red Chuck Taylors crunched the gravel.

Mr. de Luca made a face at Josh before he stepped out.

"Thank you for buying this for me." Josh's flabby arm raised the spiral notebook. "I appreciate it."

"You're welcome." Mrs. de Luca dabbed her eyes. "You need to make notes, Mr. Actor. We want you to be good. I want you to do it."

"Don't forget your lube and protection."

"Reggie!"

"You need another line drive to the face!" Josh mimed bobbling a hard shot to shortstop after being hit in the eye and crying. "Maybe you'll catch it this time and not blow the game."

Reggie flung his body across the back seat. "I'm not the one getting balls to the face today!"

The tractor stopped; its door swung open. The driver plopped his short, stocky frame—hemmed in by faded blue jeans, a flannel shirt, and a thick, brown jacket with tan patches on the elbows—out of the cabin and walked over the squishy ground to the main gate. The collie scampered over and wagged its tail. Josh offered his palm, which the dog's nose rubbed.

"You must be Josh."

"I am. Hi."

"Pete Moynihan, but you can call me Bud."

The two shook hands, and Josh noticed the warmth and weight of the farmer's hand—not a crushing grip, not an intimidating grip, but more like a block of solid wood not easily moved. Josh stuffed his hand back in his pockets. He reluctantly wished he had listened to Janis and brought his jacket. She was right: The air in the country was crisper, open—no skyscrapers and city blocks as shields.

Farmer Bud threw his hands onto his hips. "Great day for a tour. Couldn't ask for better weather. I bet, though, we get one more pass of snow. April is a funny month. The trees are coming back online. Birds are flying about. We got babies coming. Some flowers out." His arm bounced along the horizon broken up by trees and spurts of colors. "But somehow all this gets teased. One more hard snow, I bet. That's my wife Lydia over there." Farmer Bud waved to a tall, strong-looking woman wearing a denim shirt, jeans, and hiking boots. She waved back and turned a garden hose toward metal boxes strewn between the house and dirt paths linking the outbuildings. "We're glad you're here. Ready?"

"Uh…yeah," Josh mumbled, hiking his khakis up over his belly and rolling the notebook like a newspaper into his chubby hand.

Behind him, a family of geese and goslings and mallard ducks paraded by and honked at the station wagon squeaking toward the entrance road, under the sign, and disappearing into the trees leading to the highway.

"We're a family-owned operation," Farmer Bud said as they took a left near paddocks where herds of cows dotted the fields—some standing, some lying down, some mooing. "My grandfather, also a Pete, started this after he got to this side of the country. His family knew dairy, ran one outside Cleveland, and had come from a long line of dairy farmers back in the old country. Match made in heaven." He stopped by a metal railing. "The ladies in here are on a break. Maternity leave."

Josh reached for his pen and notebook.

"Dry cows." Farmer Bud pointed to the fenced-off pasture. "Sixty days before they calve and lactate. They relax, focus on their new babies. We put the mothers out here after the calves have been born. They drink so much of their mamas' milk. It's like telling a kid to lay off candy. But the cows roam free. I know each and every one."

"Really?" Josh fumbled with his notebook as he looked over the black and white spots and velvety brown smudges. The smell nauseated him.

One of the mid-sized cows lumbered over to the rail, and Farmer Bud jostled a yellow tag in the cow's ear before blowing kisses at her. "Some we can tell right away by their markings or how they move or their personality. We have a lot. Tags help."

The round sophomore looked at the tag—ABIGAIL. Josh smiled and scribbled in his notebook until Abigail farted and returned to chewing grass.

"A dairy cow, on average, weighs about fourteen hundred pounds, but Ayrshires and Jerseys can weigh up to two thousand. The Guernsey is a great dairy breed, and Jersey cows produce high-fat milk perfect for butter, ice cream, cheese, yogurt."

"What do you do each day?"

"Each day is pretty much the same, save for some surprises. We milk twice a day. Morning and afternoon. Rain or shine…or snow. We start early in the morning, usually around four. My daughter and her husband will rinse the milker and set up the parlor back there." Farmer Bud pointed to the large building. "While one of us, usually me, wakes up the ladies and starts moving them to the holding paddock. Once there, we start feeding. We feed them all kinds of good stuff, depending on their dietary needs, their weight, and milk-production levels. Grain, oats, some hay, corn, soybean meal, malted rye."

"Does that come out in the milk? I mean, can you taste it?"

"No. But if we mix in pieces of chocolate, they produce chocolate milk." He looked down at Josh's pen wiggling. "Just kidding. Don't write that. It's not true. Honestly, this is the boring stuff in some ways. Let's check out the feed barn, the milking parlor, and we'll see the machines and meet our hard-working ladies up close."

Josh rerolled his notebook and clipped the pen onto the spiral.

As they walked, Farmer Bud asked, "What's this for again?"

"A school project."

"Science?"

"A play. I'm the milkman."

"Ah. Keeping it real."

They walked over a dirt trail, between the silos, and into the big metal building—open-air on three sides and squat V-shaped roof—where some cows stood in fenced-off alleys. The whole area was clean except for years of use and debris clinging to support beams, railings, and walls.

"When it's time for milking, we bring them in here, feed them, hook them up, milk, send the milk to the main storage tank, clean them up, send them back out to the field, and they go about their day." Farmer Bud shrugged. "And that's that."

"That's that." Josh looked around the large building churning out farm and machinery sounds and the smells of large hoofed mammals. Hay, mud, and dung littered the alleys. He quickly opened his notebook.

"It takes about ten minutes. We milk one hundred cows. After about three hours, milking is done. One person sanitizes the milker, and another of us closes the parlor after tidying up. One hundred cows can make a mess. We wash the whole parlor with a pressure washer so it's ready for the afternoon milking, which is about to happen." Farmer Bud motioned to a young woman tucking her hair under a stocking cap and lining up cows from the paddocks and into the parlor. "After the parlor is clean, the cows are let out to the pasture, and we humans get our second breakfast before we enjoy our free time…ha ha ha…

which includes non-milking chores. We feed grain and hay to the oldest calves. We rotate fields for grazing. We'll give our neighbors a heads-up when manure-application day is on its way. You don't want to be having a party or a cookout that day."

Josh drilled an asterisk into the paper.

"We repair or build fences, upkeep machinery, maintain the paddocks…and take care of the chickens, horses, cats, and dogs. And then, we're back at it at around four in the afternoon. Same song and dance. The cows are brought into the parlor and wait their turn. We're done by seven in the evening, give or take. Everything is washed down and dried. The parlor closed up. We double-check the gates to make sure nobody has gotten out. We get some dinner, family time, and sleep. There's not a day off for anybody here. Most family farms don't have too many employees…just the family."

"Every day?"

"Every day. If you come over here, I can show you what's next for us."

Josh followed Farmer Bud toward a bulky metal box bolted into an unscathed concrete floor; its flat, wide roof was taller than both of them, and it had no dents, no trace of mud or manure, and looked like an amalgamation of structures and components from an automatic car wash, an industrial-sized elevator, a section of a jetway leading to an airplane, and a supercomputer. Electrical wires and hydraulic pumps zigzagged along the sides. Turnstiles, the kind Josh had walked through at sports events and concerts, snaked around the main blue and silver unit. The apparatus had a presence to it, as though it was a central nervous system or a giant motherboard connecting, channeling, and redistributing power throughout the farm. The whole thing hummed.

"This is the future." Farmer Bud tapped his hand onto a computer screen buried in the middle of a panel of glowing amber buttons with one giant green switch and one giant red switch.

The screen flickered gray and then bright off-white, reminding Josh of a television turning on. HELLO! WELCOME TO LACTEC RMS. PLEASE ENTER YOUR PASSWORD.

Farmer Bud punched a combination of letters and numbers on the touchscreen's keyboard. "This is a Robotic Milking System, and we're testing it."

Josh scribbled away.

"With the old way of milking, we'd have to wash the teats by hand and get a few squirts going before we could attach the automatic milkers. But with the robot…"

"Robot?"

"Down here." Farmer Bud's knees cracked. "This arm can detect if the udder is ready." He tapped a long gray rod extending into a black and silver box—no bigger than four decks of cards stacked atop each other—capped on the end and covered with triangular warning stickers amplified in the middle with graphics of electric bolts. "The robot is faster, more efficient, and the cow can be milked when she's ready. She is free to come and go as she pleases. No coaxing from us. Before this, we'd spend a lot of time prepping and milking and cleaning… standing in the pit to do it."

"The *robot* starts the milking process," Josh's voice faded. He had not written for several minutes.

"It monitors her health, her chewing rate, her movement, you name it. Handiest piece of equipment we've bought in years…costliest, too. But it'll save us time and money. It'll take a lot of pressure off my wife, my children, and me. The cow enters an individual stall like our current parlor." Farmer Bud thumbed toward the lower level and the alleys filled with cows behind him. "And the machine reads her collar for all her information. Is she ready? Is it not time yet? I can check flow rates and manage the software from a computer, tablet, or my smart phone. Give it a minute here, and you'll see it in action."

One of the cows entered the machine's gates, which buzzed open until the cow was inside and then buzzed closed. A feeder lowered to the cow's shins and, after a thin red laser beam shone across her collar, jostled back up until it stopped under the chin; the cow lumbered forward and started munching. Farmer Bud swiveled his phone in the air and showed Josh a pale blue box with the name MISS FANTASIA in it, along with her tag number, how much milk she provided on an average daily basis, and how much she provided last time. The robot arm whirred from its nest along the low end of the main box, straightened out, pointing toward the gate on the other side of Miss Fantasia, slid under her udder, and flipped over. Before the robot could attach to the udder, Miss Fantasia kicked the arm four times, her powerful right hoof flinging brown goop close to Farmer Bud and Josh and snapping the arm back; the arm retreated, recalculated, re-approached, at which time the bulky Jersey stomped the robotic end whizzing like a remote-controlled car.

"She's still getting used to it," Farmer Bud said, chuckling.

More feed bulleted down, and Miss Fantasia stuck her head in the feeder. With the cow calmer and more interested in the oats, the robot tried again and attached to the udder.

"Teat sanitation. Warm water, air, stimulating for pre-milking, and…" Farmer Bud waited a few seconds. "Now drying. The robot can adjust to high, low, wide, and other irregularities in teats."

"Irregularities in teats," Josh repeated, thinking of Reggie. "The robot knows?"

"Mmm."

MILKING PERMITTED flashed on the main computer screen; a few seconds later Farmer Bud's phone dinged with the same message. Milk gurgled from clear tubes winding from the main unit to bottles stationed nearby.

"The robot can detect abnormal milk and divert it," he explained.

A generator hummed in the room behind them.

"When she's done, the robot re-sanitizes, the stall opens, and off she goes. It's pretty much how we do it now…just a robot will be taking over. We'll see the results of everybody's hard work…cows *and* humans in the main tank room. Plus, the goodies are in the refrigerators in there."

Miss Fantasia gave one more swift kick to the robot arm retreating beneath her, waited for the exit gate to open, and went on her way.

The robot returned with a nozzle, hosed down the floor, steam and suds rising, and washed mud, manure, and other debris down the floor drain.

Farmer Bud put away his phone and punched the keypad on the unit's computer. "We got a surrogacy through AI, and the robot can detect who's ready to be a mom. We can tell…those bodily signs they have…but the robot makes sure we're right."

Josh stared at the robot arm retracting like a mechanical serpent into its chrome and aluminum lake. "Artificial intelligence?"

"Artificial insemination. We don't have a bull here." Farmer Bud glanced down. "Do you need to know this kind of stuff for your play?"

Josh kept writing, and as he did, his eyes wandered from the paper and the ink, surveyed the lines of cows, and kept returning to the machine dominating the middle of the parlor—its low hum resonated on his skin. The whole thing reminded him of science-fiction stories and a hospital room's web of devices. He started reading those stories—machines coming to life, machines taking over, machines having a soul, machines replacing humans, tools becoming the masters—after his mother was pulled from life support. The leaves had reached full fall foliage, and the brilliant colors outside the hospital window countered the room's palette of washed-out whites, fluorescent yellows, and digital greens. A letter—his father had told him to write, get down his thoughts, and read it to her, looking like she couldn't listen, with all the wires hooked into her, her eyes closed, her breathing regulated, but she would hear him, his father promised. Josh sat by the edge of the bed: one flick of a switch, he noticed—her pulse dimming. He unfolded his letter but couldn't finish reading aloud; the words reached her, he believed, but she could not receive them. She was no longer dependent on a thing knowing her only by her vital signs—a sequence of those signs and their maximal and minimal efficiency; a thing that did not and could never wholly know her vitality. Her body accelerated further from the machine and from him; her body, freed from suspension, finally answering the question it had repeatedly asked since her prognosis: Where is the way out?

He looked up at Farmer Bud—the question of what does and does not matter with regards to a minor role in a play, such as his—and shrugged. "I don't know," he replied as an electrified wind chilled the air.

"I guess it might be good to have." Farmer Bud tapped the yellow notebook. "You know, something that may be of use, my dad and his dad drove their delivery truck all over this area to deliver fresh goods."

"Did they wear the white uniform with a black bowtie and a hat?"

"They sure did. They had the bowtie and the uniforms with our name and Gracie on it, who looks pretty much the same now as she did all those years ago. We're thinking about bringing that back…the old uniforms everyone knows by heart."

"That might be cool."

"I agree. People remember that sort of thing. Hey, maybe your costume could be that."

"I've asked Ms. Rollins about it. She's not in charge of that. Darcy is." Josh stopped writing, glanced at the parlor's outermost edges encircling animals and metal and trees and sky, but returned to the machine in the middle.

Farmer Bud opened a large freezer door and pulled out a small carton of ice cream and a plastic spoon. "Here's a sample for you to take home. We started adding some flavors to the milk. Coffee. Strawberry. This is my favorite."

"Root beer?" Josh exclaimed, looking at the carton with Grandpa Pete—ball cap pushed back; hands across his plaid shirt—and Gracie the Moynihan Dairy cow—front hooves over her udder; derby tilted to the side—smiling in rocking chairs on a porch.

"When's the big night for the play?"

"Before school's out. May."

"You'll have to let me know how you did."

The station wagon pulled into the flat patch of grass where it had stopped hours ago; Reggie leaned over his father and tapped the horn three quick times. The collie's ears perked up, and cows in the paddock looked over their shoulders.

Farmer Bud stuck out his hand and shook Josh's. "Good luck, young man. It was a pleasure meeting you, and thank you for touring our farm. What flavors would they like?"

"No, that's all right. It's just my dad and brother." Josh glanced at Janis. "She's not my mom. Thanks."

He took his carton and walked out of the large building until he slid into the station wagon's back seat where he fended off Reggie's fingers digging at the carton and the yellow notebook. His brother reeked of cologne and had unbuttoned his shirt low enough for the few sprigs of his chest hair, which meant he would be picking up his girlfriend Tabitha when they got home. The radio was low, and his father's hand rubbed his wife's knee. The collie escorted them out; when the station wagon reached the frontage road, the Moynihan Dairy sign swinging over them, the dog turned back.

Janis looked over her shoulder like a swan. "How was it?"

"OK," Josh answered, knowing that anyone in the car could have asked him how it went but that she would be the one who did.

• • •

After an early dinner, Mr. de Luca drove Josh to school and dropped him off near the parking lot behind the auditorium. Other cars idled in front of the station wagon, and out popped other cast members, waving goodbye, blowing kisses, and heading inside. Janis had asked Josh if he wanted any of his favorite meals as a break-a-leg good-luck charm for his big night. Yes, he begrudgingly agreed to his step-mom's offer, part of him hoping this would alleviate some of the aching pretense she was anything but his dad's new wife. Another part of him hoped these kinds of yeses to her would be a middle ground between them and the lands they each respectively occupied in the house and in life— hers filled with household and personal goods imported from Europe, donating time and money to philanthropic endeavors, and running her consulting business, all while, she said, "never losing sight of family and what's important"; his scrambled with family memories, a recent acquisition of dairy-production knowledge, and completing a class requirement of standing in front of an audience for a play, for which she was cheering him on while fixing his preferred sandwich, side, and dessert.

He didn't know how to stop Janis from spreading into more segments of his life—this one being the foods his mom fixed and the gastronomical bonds they had. Janis continued to distinguish herself from his mom: Declaring her age never embarrassed her whenever someone asked, and she never showed remorse about being forty-seven and older than his dad; she could effortlessly balance work and life; and she was outgoing and fashionable and everyone seemed to know her, which strengthened after she became a member of the family, after all those dates Mr. de Luca took her on, after they met at a support group for survivors of terminally ill patients.

Before Josh left for the performance, Janis repeated how proud she was of him; how, if this was his one time on stage, it would a good thing—his mom would be proud of him. He glared at her when she mentioned his mom; a cold sadness covered him as quickly as anger had. "I'll be front row and center. I can't wait," she said. She would sit next to his father, and this would not be the first time they had sat together at a school function for either son, but the play was different and constricted inside Josh. And he said yes to her request about his favorite foods before his performance, trying to be more accommodating, after he and his dad had yet another talk, the last one after the trip to the dairy, about the way things were in the de Luca household and what was expected of him. He thanked her for taking the time from her regular Sunday evening to fix his favorite meal.

"See you back here," his dad said before driving home.

With the grilled-cheese-and-ham sandwich, potato chips, and a bowl of strawberries topped with whipped cream and candied walnuts in his stomach, Josh trudged toward the green room where Darcy verified costumes. She checked off his name and a series of boxes next to it when she handed a cap, a loose beige shirt like long johns, and suspenders for Acts One and Two, before reminding him he was responsible for finding her during intermission to claim his cold-weather wardrobe. He held up a pair of dark corduroy jeans Janis had bought, after she overheard him telling his dad that the pair Darcy had for him didn't feel comfortable, and asked if it would be OK to wear. He assumed she would nix it and waited for her to add "with all that research you did, this?"

But the spritely junior adjusted her glasses. "Try 'em on." And after he did, she motioned to his bright silver buckle. "Ditch the belt. Suspenders only, and you're good." She spun around to her rack and lint-rolled a Victorian-era dress with a brooch on its collar.

Josh grabbed the black galoshes flopped near the wardrobe bins and made his way to the long table and its mirror and lights. He sat in a plastic chair and set out the instructions, written by Darcy, for applying his makeup to resemble an early-1900s dairy farmer in his fifties. He added deep lines to his jowl and by his eyes. He dabbed his left cheek as she had showed him—"Stubble only"—with the foam applicator and the tub of dark makeup paint. He rolled his sleeves above his elbow, slapped his suspenders over his shoulders, and set the cap atop his puffy dark hair.

Returning with leggings and an apron, Darcy said, "You look the part."

"Yeah?" Josh looked at the mirror and pretended setting his character's metal basket of milk bottles next to him. He flattened his script, reviewed Act One's lines, and skipped to Act Three and his entrance. He had circled that page—his character's last appearance—and, after many weeks ignoring it, realized this.

• • •

During rehearsals Josh wondered why he was doing this —for a grade he was required to participate in the play; a requirement Ms. Rollins reminded him when he asked if he could write a detailed minimum-ten-page essay on whatever theme she was willing to assign him or one about which he felt strongly after observing (*"observing* practice" he emphasized to her) what was happening on stage, highlighting in his plea that her paper assignments typically ran no more than four or five pages.

"Nice try, Mr. de Luca. But the syllabus requires contribution to the year-end play with acting or backstage help." She showed him the list of remaining cast and crew. "Anything catch your fancy?"

"No, not really."

"You like research, right?"

"Yeah."

"And you like to learn new things, right?"

"Yeah."

"Do you think you can find out about life as a dairy farmer in early twentieth-century New England?"

Josh shrugged. "I guess. Yeah."

"I bet there are real working farms in the area. You could talk to someone, visit, get some ideas of what that job is like. Listen, this is your chance to add a little something to the character. Why don't we compromise this way? I need a dairy farmer in all the acts, and you can find out what all that entails. There aren't many lines. You're probably on stage for a total of ten minutes for all three acts. Sound fair?"

"I guess."

"Well, thank you, Mr. de Luca, and congratulations." She leaned closer to him. "You're my Harold Newman, dairy farmer of Grimes Corner, Vermont."

Dairy farmer or *milkman*, as the script's cast of characters called him. Josh had wondered if there was as difference—if so, how and what? He had no idea what either of those names involved. Maybe the latter was an antiquated name for a career; the former for something more recent, elaborate, and dependent on more than vintage photos of cows and churn buckets and horse-drawn carriages. But he then saw the two terms were interchangeable. *Dairy farmer* was no more regal or more suggestive of acres of land ownership than *milkman* and its singular-sounding function; one was the other, and both were the same. Having realized this, he did not feel defeated because he hadn't tried out for the role but was strong-armed into taking it, which was for a grade for a class he didn't care about.

When Janis found out about his role, she was elated, telling Josh this was a way for him to channel energy and some emotion and do something creative and expressive. "You'll have to make me believe you're a dairy farmer. It would get your mind off things…being someone else for a while. You could have fun with it, too. You can do it. I know you can."

That night Josh powered on his computer and searched for dairy+farms+Denver+Boulder and found several, including the goat farm La Chèvre de Flatirons, but Moynihan Dairy won him over because of its About Us and History links. MD was the only farm promoting tours of the property, and according to the map, they were close enough for a Saturday afternoon excursion, which would not require asking Reggie to take him—which he would do but would deliberately be late in picking him up until

Josh would think he would have to hitchhike home or, Reggie had goaded in the past, accept a ride in a stranger's van with FREE HUGS INSIDE spray painted on the windowless doors.

"What's that?" Reggie asked, dropping his baseball glove and athletic cup on Josh's desk.

"School work."

"This too?" He tapped the second tab of the browser.

"I'm in a play for class."

"Are you?" Reggie's tone strained at its uppermost range as he smirked.

Josh spun toward the second tab's search results of acting+techniques, clicking it closed, and expected insults.

"Cool. Congrats. I couldn't do that." Reggie texted on his phone before continuing. "I mean, I could and be awesome at it, but it's not my thing." He slapped Josh on the shoulder before heading for the shower.

Josh waited until he heard his older brother cycling through his usual shower songs—leap-frogging from hip-hop to classic-rock standards and pausing in order to text—and then, upon hearing these starts and stops in between the curtain sliding open and closed, returned to the second tab. Hundreds of websites devoted space to various acting techniques. Less than thirty lines, less than ten minutes, he reminded himself about Ms. Rollins's estimate. He bypassed a series of audio and video courses, distance-learning downloads, and media requiring purchases and opted for a few blogs by actors he did not know but who claimed to have worked with the "best directors, entertainers, and professionals in the industry."

Immersing himself in the basics of method acting, memory fillers, and imaginative introspection—techniques ranging from inventing a character's back story to using the actor's personal experiences—as well as spending time in historical societies' online archives and on websites of dairy farms on the Atlantic coast, of which there were plenty, and setting a day and time to visit Moynihan Dairy, Josh felt more than prepared for the play, his role, and Ms. Rollins's expectations.

After-school rehearsals in the auditorium in March were mostly half-lit because Ms. Rollins wanted a low-key feel for practice and the emotional space. She was militaristic with her commands—what to do; where to go; errors—and as rehearsals compounded, this class requirement contorted into hard labor and punishment once the end-of-school bell rang. Josh was reminded why he didn't want to do this in the first place yet could not opt out, and he hoped afternoon after afternoon that Reggie had not left baseball practice without him, which would force him to ask for a ride from the students affiliated with drama productions who could say their lines with confidence in an otherworldly magic.

Ms. Rollins lobbed around the term *minimalism* and explained the play's lack of details and number of props. Everything within Grimes Corner was suggestive, sparse, and left to the imagination—a place and its events condensed, which made Josh wonder why he was researching and planning a visit to a real dairy farm. His time and effort could be for naught, an illusion if the space around him was stripped to the essentials.

Read-throughs of the script were scheduled in the weeks before spring break, which, Ms. Rollins said, was a great opportunity for the characters to immerse themselves in their lines and their places—literally and figuratively—in the play. Josh glanced at a few of his lines in Act One but became distracted and didn't bother reading the whole acts in which his character arrived. After spring break, the first time he had lines on stage for rehearsal he choked, referring multiple times to the script. Rehearsals became a place where he could not ignore what was happening in front of him with the themes and the characters saying what they were saying at the time they were speaking— their dialogues charged with personal meaning.

"Do you know how milk is made, Josh?" Ms. Rollins asked loudly during the weeks of blocking.

"Yeah, I've been to a farm. I know about it. I've seen it. Machines do it all now. It's one big robot."

Sections of the stage, standing on their marks, snickered; sections of the dark auditorium giggled.

"What do you think is in those bottles?" Ms. Rollins pointed to a blank space near him.

Josh looked down at his empty hands. He couldn't see bottles or milk.

"Show us."

Sighing, Josh set down an invisible bottle at the feet of the student playing Mrs. West who had asked Harold Newman if he had an extra bottle of cream for the upcoming wedding between her daughter and the Bibbs's boy.

"Did it clink?"

"What?"

"Is it glass? Is it plastic? Is grass or concrete under it?"

"Really?" he mumbled.

"I beg your pardon, Mr. de Luca." Ms. Rollins paced the front of the stage. "Do you how much a draft horse weighs, one that would bring a town fresh dairy products every day?"

"The farm I went to has delivery vans."

"Don't get smart, Josh."

"Besides, you said I wouldn't have a real horse. It's all make-believe. It's minimalist."

"You *don't* have a real horse, but you need to *show* us you do."

Josh puffed out his cheeks and flipped through his practice script until a door at the back of the auditorium opened. Snow danced in the bright bluish light as it fell outside his room when Janis brought him a mug of hot cocoa late one night. "Mom put marshmallows in Reggie's, not mine," he snapped at her. She returned a few minutes with fresh mug.

"You should find out," Ms. Rollins continued. "Then you can give us a much better performance than what you are now. Make us believe a horse is behind you, you are pulling that old nag from your barn over a road and toward town, and *that horse* has a cart behind her, probably wooden…unless you can show me the 1900s had metal carts. And so she's pulling, and it's filled with your daily deliveries. What's the line there where we are… toward the middle, your line?"

"Cream and milk."

"A difference in the two."

"I know."

"Good. You deliver an important food product, Josh. You're a staple of this town. You are in every act doing the same thing. Do you get that?"

"Yes."

"Do you understand the symbolism of this role?"

"Yes."

"Do you?"

He shrugged.

"You're dealing with animals that are muddy and dirty. You're doing a demanding thing. And you do it every day."

"I know. I've seen that up close."

"Tap into that. You're a big factor in this community. Stability and order. You represent mundane, everyday life. You are present every morning, as sure as the sun rises." Ms. Rollins sat down in the front row and dragged a large three-ring binder into her lap. "Somebody made that milk without the technology we have now. This isn't you getting a bottle of milk after going to the grocery store with your parents waiting in the car. You've done that research."

Leading up to dress rehearsal, weeks away from the first public performance, Josh had not understood why Ms. Rollins talked about the town and its inhabitants cycling through life and what remains are neither memories nor images but ghosts, unfulfilled wishes, and lost hopes; she repeated the word *regret* until Josh felt he could apply it to being on stage and not behind the scenes. I could've handled the money and the tickets, he thought, standing in full costume under the warm lights, his pants itching, makeup burning his cheeks, Ms. Rollins offering her last-minute critiques. I'm real good with Excel. Way better than Reg. Ms. Rollins returned to the themes of family and time—the past and *carpe diem* but never the future—the dead do all they can to get the living's attention. Time's tide was heaviest in the past where it pushed and pulled at fathoms before tapering out like froth the farther it loosened and broke away.

None of this sunk into him until the last full dress rehearsal. During the times he dry-practiced Act Three, the dialogue and the scene did not impact him; Act Three and his small role as a flashback was no different than the read-throughs and the blocking—like a body dressed and talking but not moving, not charged. But as he listened and watched from stage right, he realized the dead spoke during this act and they wanted to be with the living and in the daily comings and goings of the town and all those attached to it; realized the past could not happen again, no matter how badly it was wished for and spoken about. A thing from the past cannot be undone; the dead recall events and moments, which they could talk about with each other and which they carried with them as they sat upright like pale stones in the graveyard of the town.

Josh's father had made the decision to end his mother's life support and had conferred with his sons beforehand. "This is not a life," he said, explaining why life was more than an exchange of blood and oxygen, more than resting in one world while another passed like clouds over sky. "This is not a life she would want."

During rehearsal when Mrs. Bibbs spoke to her daughter-in-law Elanor West, recently placed in the graveyard but wanting to return to the living, having seen them around her—sad that she was gone at such a young age—the young mother feeling her death wasn't real, asking if she could return to the living for one day based on a memory that had never left her, Josh excused himself from the stage, slid between the two ladders representing second-floor windows of the two different homes on Main Street, through the back partition, and stepped into the parking lot behind the auditorium. He did not want his castmates seeing him cry. Choose any ordinary day, Mrs. Bibbs had said, not a sad or happy day, not the valleys or the peaks, but a commonplace day in the middle because the least important day is important enough.

• • •

"Places, everyone," the assistant director announced to the green room. "Act Three in five minutes."

Josh breathed deeply as he faced the mirror for the night's final time. He had matched his castmates' cues with a fluidity that moved the show from the early morning and daily life of Act One through the wedding between Elanor West and George Bibbs of Act Two, years later in the future. And he had flubbed only one of his lines in Act One, answering Mrs. Bibbs's question of why he was late today with "something went wrong with the robot," not with the original line's reference of "the separator"—which Josh saw in his head as the centrifugal contraption with its wood hand crank bolted on the post under the metallic bowl, having discovered an old photo of one, circa the same era as his character's—to which Michelle Yuen, tall and medical in her Victorian blouse and floor-length dress, smiled graciously and rolled with the his slip. Both acts had him start offstage, his voice calling out to his invisible horse Bessie, his body appearing from behind the curtain, tugging at the assembly-line illusion of horse pulling a cart cradling dairy. Josh dabbed a towel on his face where sweat had diluted some of the makeup, smearing the middle-age wrinkles, and reapplied more. He found Darcy and acquired his red flannel coat and hat with earflaps. Act Three was to be ten below freezing.

The curtain opened, and out came the stage manager, who, as she had in the other acts, spoke directly to the audience as a character and narrator of the play. Josh noticed the seats in front of the stage were mostly filled, but the sides had emptied, some having not refilled after intermission. He found his dad and Janis sitting front row and center as she said they would. Reggie and Tabitha had moved toward the back of the auditorium where, Josh knew, they would make out with one pair of hands and text with the other pair, leaving when the show was over. He would be out there soon enough, repeating his daily delivery and his usual dialogue with the other characters about the weather, the town, and the gossip of lives woven between.

The newly deceased Elanor West, who died in childbirth, asked the dead and the stage manager if she could go back to the living for one day—she had heard it's possible. Watching and listening, Josh pulled on his gloves. The dead and the stage manager warned her about trying this; it will only bring more heartache. Something indescribable does go on after life, they admitted, but no one has been sure what that is, and she should embrace it and wean herself off the living and the earth—let them be. Josh buttoned his flannel coat but, feeling too hot, unbuttoned it as Elanor pressed on until she got her wish—the day of her twelfth birthday, February, 1899. The lights on the other side of the stage eased on, and Elanor saw her mother in the kitchen. The stage manager set the scene for her and the audience: snow, a Tuesday, dawn, the exact start of what the young woman had asked for—the whole day. Elanor exclaimed she saw Constable Wilkerson and Harold Newman on his delivery.

His entrance cued, Josh emerged from the backstage shadows; he was more nervous than he had been. Nearer to the action, he started tugging the invisible reins, clicking his tongue, and together he and his horse stopped at the trellis of the West home. He stroked Bessie's ghostly nose and stepped to his spot where Ms. Rollins and the assistant director had blocked during practice. Mrs. West said her lines—a good morning to him as ordinary as she had greeted him in the first two acts and a comment about the bone-chilling temperature—but he did not respond. The curly redheaded senior looked at Josh and bulged her eyeballs. *Hello* her tightened face expressed. *Don't you want to respond with your lines?* After a few silent seconds, "Good mor…," Mrs. West repeated louder but stopped when Josh stepped from the play's action and closer to the front of the stage like a soliloquist.

When he stepped forward, Josh knew all eyes in front of and behind the curtain would fall on him, which they did, and, having made this move, he had to now follow through on what he had started. The stage shortened in front of him, but an edge remained, and the distance from the edge to the first row of audience members increased as the film-colored shadow widened between them and Josh. The audience sat vast, cold, and gray-blue; they waited for him to speak, which he believed he was prepared to do but had no idea what he was doing or why he stepped forward until he cleared his throat and stared into the auditorium seats.

And for a brief moment Josh believed he spoke. "Ladies and gentlemen…" And he believed in this moment, he paused again, this was happening and couldn't be stopped and that one of his castmates on stage, the assistant director backstage, or Ms. Rollins would quickly appear and stop him, usher him along, keep the play going without him. But no one did. And he continued believing he spoke. "I stand before you in the 1900s, and I come to the future to tell you of serious changes to life. Machines will take over how we live, and we will let it happen. We will give them power to do what we want from them. We will hand over so much to them, all in the name of convenience and progress. But what's the price? Tied to a machine? That machines can make life perfect? To have a machine stop death, which it can't?" Eyes tightened on him as he believed he spoke, and he wondered what would be waiting for him after the play, in the car ride home, at school the next day, if anyone would say anything, if he would be punished. "Why will we let this happen? We'll say it's the way it has to be, and we won't give it a second thought. I am asking you to ask yourselves why do we do this, why we have to keep this up? Why do we need these things to be between us and our lives when we already know the outcome?"

Out of the corner of his eye, Josh watched the assistant director fumble for the page in the script; by the time she could find it and mouth it to him, it would be too late, and he was uncertain how much time had passed with him petrified on his mark.

And then a line he had said earlier popped in his head. He rubbed his gloves together and set the invisible basket of bottles on the trellis. "Good morning, Mrs. West," he improvised, "my mind was on the weather. Bessie has been shivering all morning. Easy, girl." He patted the air where his draft horse's haunches would be. "It's ten below at my barn." After glancing upward at the rows of lights and the pretend sky over him, he pulled down the bill of his cap and pulled up the collar of his coat. "We may get more snow, but I think a fine day will burn through. See you tomorrow."

The redhead playing Mrs. West relaxed her face and body, thanked him, told him goodbye, and shivered under her shawl while he walked across Main Street, tightening his fist to lead his horse by the reins.

Before he disappeared on the other side of the stage for good, Josh glanced at the audience. He was certain he had stood at the front of the stage for a long time and said what he imagined he had said. His father's face was soft as he slouched in the chair and dozed, his caterpillar-eyebrows quiet. The two seats next to his father were empty, where Reggie and Tabitha had sat before intermission. Josh and Janis looked at each other. She smiled at him and nodded as though she were the only one who had heard him and waited for him to say more.

Crane and Hoist

Poor Joe Riggs. Time has slowed to a taffy-stretch for him while he waits for rescue, and any subtle shifts in him or in the crane could worsen the mishap. He had been looking forward to finishing the recent job for his company FRANZEN BROS. HEAVY EQUIPMENT, LLC – LET US DO THE LIFTING FOR YOU—the company name and motto emblazoned in puffy yellow letters on the sides of the cherry-red cab he is trapped in.

After kissing his wife goodbye, he climbed into his crane's cab as he had on any other day, knowing the project manager scheduled the lift for the early morning hours of a spring day when Joe loves working because of the sunrise's oranges and pinks in the blue sky and waiting, coffee on the dashboard, radio humming, for the "Raise boom" thumbs-up signal from his long-time colleague and best friend Dave Roberts, a Cherokee who nicknamed Joe "Smoke" because Joe's hair color turned gray before the age of thirty and because Joe has done worked in the air for the company—in it while operating a tower crane or through it while driving a crane truck and moving objects, with surgeon-like precision, as he did this morning. Dave figured a guy like Joe, having earned two Employee of the Year awards in his twenty-five years with the company and known for his good attitude, hard work, and insistence on being a team player, needed a nickname—a short one so Dave, who stays on and is in charge of the ground (has been, handling the radio, directions, and crew when Joe needs them), can call out to Joe. The two men laughed and thought that nickname was much better than Joe "Two Mortgages" Riggs. Sometimes Joe has worried that people on the com channel will hear the word *smoke* and worry real smoke is emitting from somewhere. This has not happened yet, and Joe has hoped this does not happen. He does not want to be accused of causing confusion.

As a vendor, Franzen Bros. is one of the area's major recipients for contracts to big and small projects, and as a long-serving veteran, Joe has worked at some of the most popular attractions and properties, such as the Historical Society and its famous domed top, which Joe and company updated by adding sheets of all-weather siding and improved flashing underneath, and points of interest considered "hidden secrets and obscure gems" by travelogues and the Internet, such as the Bill and Ruth Hansen Museum of Historic Drought, with its collection of scientific research and artifacts of the century-ago drought that ravaged the area, where Joe helped hoist key infrastructure supports from ground to the multi-level building. He has taken civic and personal pride in helping out anyway he could with these projects, mainly as Smoke lifting things in the air, and today's project—installing the giant sculpture of twisted metal for a new museum of art slated to open on Memorial Day—was a welcome task. But the morning has not turned out the way Joe expected.

Were he able to reach his phone, which, like him, is pinned between his jacket pockets and seat and, like him, won't be going anywhere until help arrives, his status update on social media would be *Help trapped*, written quickly, were he not in shock and able to calm his fingers over the keyboard, and written without concern for grammar or clear directions to anyone monitoring his social-media feed, which, at this time of day, would be his younger brother stationed in Germany, that he would have to rely on auto-correct capitalizing the h in *Help* and add the vowels in *trapped*, and he would have to rely on his Navy-employed brother moving past his initial reaction ("Ha ha Joey's complaining about the Starbucks line again.") and toward interpreting the situation and filling the gaps of the hypothetical message with the word *me*, as in *Help me*, a colon or a dash following the imperative, and the simple but complete subject-verb phrase *I am trapped in the cab of my crane*, which would beg the questions (a) Why is Joseph Daniel Riggs trapped in his much-loved and much-preferred office of choice? and (b) Why is he, not his ground crew, especially Dave Roberts, or first responders, announcing or, more importantly, rectifying it? But things being what they are for the fifty-two-year-old and his repositioned crane, neither phantasmic message nor the flesh-and-blood crane operator will be moving anywhere but a little deeper into the ground.

The big man from the southeast corner of the state, known for its fuzzy mountains, forests, rivers, and Bigfoot sightings, has already thought about his wife Roxanne (Roxy Foxy —and his nickname for her flickers past him as the backend of the crane fishtails a little more), who balances being a full-time employee in the district's unified school system and pursuing a part-time degree in speech pathology. He has thought about his children: Dennis, his sixteen-year-old son, who is understanding the hierarchies of high school, and the pressures accompanying said hierarchies, to be someone in some circle at all times; and Joy, his twenty-year-old daughter, who, at the university of her choice, thanks to a scholarship, enjoys studying molecular structures of carcinogens, specifically lung cancer, to which Joe's older sister succumbed a few years ago, in lieu of watching television with her three roommates in the small cottage a few miles from campus and affectionately known as the Butterscotch House due to its exterior paint, which Joe first saw why during Parents' Day last year—and is the color he sees intensifying as the only light streaming into his crane's sandwiched cab.

The time that it is taking—from the beginning of the accident to its stunning and social media–worthy completion; the cab thudding into the ground outside the museum's south wall; and waiting for the ground crew to realize that the accident was impossible to stop but also not impossible to gawk at—feels long to the man trapped inside, much longer than something of this magnitude and seriousness should feel like: The counterweights attached to the crane's back and hoist were not enough, were miscalculated for the morning job, and contributed to the crane hinging forward like a trap door springing up after the lift commenced. Joe heard screaming and shouting outside the cab as metal creaked, like the lids on trash dumpsters, and when the crane started toppling and he noticed in the side mirrors the outriggers uprooting from the grass and dirt, Joe killed the procedure, but not in time, and said to himself, *Ah nuts, I am being lifted off the ground and am headed straight into…* Some quick-fire synapses inside the primal area of his brain wanted him to jump out and roll to safety, like the actors in the training videos that he had to watch for certification long ago, but Joe feared the crane could turn on its nose and fall to the side, crushing him underneath, especially if he did not roll quickly or if his steel-toed boots slowed him as he ran (he is "fit as a fiddle"—his doctor's words—and has outlived his parents). The fifty-two-year-old tightened his seatbelt, the X-shaped harness squeezing his torso; slapped his hardhat on his head as low as it would compress; heard the words "Hang on, buddy" squawking from Dave; gripped the seat's armrests; and watched the pastel-colored light recede to the gray concrete of the south wall as the morning burst one final time on the sculpture's crate swinging on the hook before plummeting into dark green grass consuming any light remaining outside the front windshield. Joe could not do or change anything. Seconds after the cab planted itself into the ground, he had a flashback of his football-playing days in high school and the many times his face was impaled into the turf thanks to a surprise tackle or being blindsided in the wrong place at the wrong time—like today.

His second thought was a run-on kindled with panic, uncertainty, and hyper-awareness floating around and looping his body:

I am facing the windshield buried in the grass, the only light I see is the sunrise coming into what would be the passenger's side window, it is butterscotch-colored, but my truck has toppled forward so that that window has cracked, and its frame is bent like a wire hanger, I am securely buckled in my chair, my hardhat remains on, the ceiling is much lower and slopes toward the broken windshield and dark green ground, I am aware of a few injuries, one is my lip is cut or maybe my mouth is cut, I taste blood, not a lot of it, but blood is in my mouth, I also taste something like engine lubricant, oil, it is not a good taste, the other injury is a lot of injuries piled into each other, my whole body aches and is on fire in certain areas, my wrist feels out of place, my thighs have twisted, my back hurts, a spot between my left shoulder blade and neck where my seatbelt snapped me in place burns a lot, I do not think that I am dead, I do not know what that would be like because as the joke goes the people who die can't tell us they're dead, that was a joke my daughter told me who heard it from her teacher in her pre-med class, it has stuck with me ever since, I hear a beeping inside the cab, and what I know of this model, that sound is probably the emergency cut-off telling me that the engine and the electrical panels have been cut off, I hope so, I do not smell gasoline, I do not smell a fire, but my pants are wet, I may have pissed myself, my coffee cup may have spilled on me, I do not see anyone coming for me yet, I hear the radio static, they are saying my name, Smoke, Joe, it's Dave, Smoke, Joe, it's Dave, Dave, I wish I could answer, I think I hear them calling for an ambulance, if I am not dead then I am close to blacking out, it has a numbing effect on me, my mouth is numb, I can feel the tingling in my legs and arms, and the tingle makes its way up to my neck, and it feels like a brain freeze after eating ice cream, I have been blinking rapidly, and my eyes are dry, or I am crying, it is hard to tell, I wish I could unbuckle the seatbelt and slide myself out of the cab, but

I can tell out of the corner of my eye that the driver's side door is closer to the ground than the passenger's door which makes me wonder if the cab is starting to sway to the left losing its balance because its rear is sticking in the air, I cannot see the jib or the hook block or if the artwork is still there and all right, I cannot see the artwork, I hope that it did not drop, I did drop the peanut butter jar in here a few weeks ago while waiting for Dave to give me the go-ahead for those pallets of steel girders, I think I can smell it, it's funny to me that I can smell that, it's also funny that I can smell the pine air freshener in here, maybe both things mean that I am not dead, I tell myself things could be much worse, I hope that I am not dead.

For the man trapped inside, this moment accumulates painful lethargy and stalls between start and finish, floating effortlessly thanks to outside forces and momentum and waiting on the energy of things having moved and of things waiting to be moved like a pendulum keeping time by circling the minutes, knocking each peg down until another minute passes for Joe Riggs who keeps his optimism and patience stimulated by imagining newscasters gathering onsite: "The newest attraction at the art museum wasn't the art but a toppled piece of heavy equipment that left a lot of onlookers *craning* to see it." He clenches his eyes, tears building in the corners; imaginary onlookers take photos, text, and call; and he adds: "The operator trapped inside the vehicle was pulled to safety and is in good condition."

The artwork tiptoes across Joe's mind as he waits trapped in the gap between past and present expanding the longer rescue arrives. The job was simple and straightforward, and he could have executed it in his sleep, which he often did, including the dream in which he carried animals to shore from a capsized boat. After weeks of helping with the new building's construction, Joe would gently lift the final piece from ground to the middle of the art garden near the museum's roof. Once the main funnel-shaped base was secured, Joe could then lift the accompanying pieces attached to the outside of the main base; these pieces included miniature metal trees, cars, cows, and street signs frozen in their swirl around the artistic nod to a notorious natural occurrence in the region and the upcoming exhibition associated with said meteorological effect—*In a Tizzy: The Weather and Emotions.*

Setting the sculpture by mid-morning and installing it by lunch were the two main goals. Museum staff could sign off and Franzen Bros. could remain on standby, per contract, if additional changes were needed. After further onsite inspections and a last-minute discussion between Franzen Bros. representatives and the museum's director, curator, and exhibitions installer—the latter asking for additional Styrofoam padding inside the crate (were the crate to rock against the sculpture during the stress of the lift) as well as asking for secondary hooks should the first set of hooks fail—phone calls were made to the participating agencies and individuals handling indemnities for the lift and the artwork upon reassessment.

Adding her opinion to the matter at hand was the artist invited to the installation and who had been born in the state but had opted for the coasts, occupying one or the other at some point in her life, but she had maintained, she told interviewers, a "nostalgic love and carefree childhood innocence" of her home state and was more than willing, perhaps too willing, critics noted, to take funds and return later with something that the good citizens could say art indeed creates empathy, engages critically, and transcends identities and metaphorical and literal boundaries. But after she revealed her creation, the news, blogs, the talk of the towns followed with scathing disapproval—the most popular and most shared being that the sculpture soon to crown the art garden looked less like a rumbling tornado (a moment striking sublimity into the hearts and minds of anyone seeing it) and more like "a lump of silver poop with things sticking from its sides plopped atop a roof." Joe chuckled at the controversy and knew focusing on his job would be healthier and more productive; he wanted to be of good use.

The green light was given; Dave nodded; Joe fired up the engine (he was not responsible for determining the counterweight). No one during the installation expressed any concern. The ground crew, along with help from the museum staff, hooked the wooden crate to the hoist and reinforced the move by swaddling the crate in industrial-strength blankets and straps. A secondary hook was used on the hoist block. No warning sounds beeped from the control box; no dangerous RPMs flashed from digital black to red; the hoist engine continued revving. Joe raised the boom enough before moving to the next portion of the lift like a mountain climber conquering a rock face step by step. He paused the motor and waited for the crate to stop swaying, and when it did, Joe engaged the motor from neutral to drive. As the crate gained height and made its way toward workers standing on the roof, the morning sunlight gleamed across Joe's face, and the warmth rewarded him for merely being in the cab and working in the morning: how it meant a great deal to him—to be there and not anywhere else—a sentiment he first felt when he operated a tower crane and could see many people below walking like ants on the cleared-off sidewalks and salted streets and when he thought, Cliché and thought how true it was—the muffled sounds in a tower; clouds in the distance breaking up and moving across the blue sky; a glistening February sun turning the snow underneath into mirrors; how far off the land could be observed; the clues the sky can send; the sky with its grotesqueness and its grace; storms having to pass through before rainbows appear—these things sharing the air.

But the crate sank quickly, and the truck tilted forward. Dave rapidly yelled "Stop!" The brief moments of reduced noise Joe loves while working—the door closed, the hum of the motor, the compressed air—were annihilated by invisible, unstoppable momentum and shouts from the roof and the ground with its mad tides of hands and arms waving and fleeing the scene as the truck pulled itself from the ground.

And now he is waiting, caught in these hours-like seconds until the crew trickles back to the site of the flopped crane after they scampered away and sought shelter as it flipped.

From the corner of his eye, Joe watches shadows jitter across the ground brightening with the rising sun. His hearing returns after tinnitus briefly smothered his ears. The blackout effect has washed away, and he stares at the cracked front windshield buried in the butterscotch-tinted grass. He has spit out more than blood.

But he cannot see police unspooling yellow tape around the scene while smoke and an engine sputters over the gathering crowds. Nor can he see an ambulance pulling in, lights on, no siren; a fire truck a few seconds behind. Another crane is on its way to stabilize Joe's—and to free the man trapped inside.

But no one has reached his window yet. The radio fell from its charger on the dashboard and landed somewhere; Joe hears his buddy's voice echoing around him, but he can't answer. Be calm, be calm, he chants to himself. At the mercy of others and at the mercy of larger forces, he wonders about the rescue procedure and why it's taking long. He sits there, like a miner stuck in a cave-in, and waits for the present to catch up to the lapse—has to wait for the gap between the present and the past to heal.

As the crane teeters forward a little more, the long crack in the front windshield spreads with seismic shifts, and Joe imagines the one fantasy that has stayed with him all these years —of taking the crane and rolling it through the downtown streets like a giant monster knocking over old buildings. He begins to accept the appropriateness of him dying at work—maybe this is his time, his check-out from Earth, a check-in at the Pearly Gates, and St. Peter double-checking his name. These things glide past him when he winces and as every second of the outside world's inactivity peels away.

But in this gap between climax and dénouement, between accident and resolution, a bird arrives and follows the gooey tightrope strung between then and now. The bird lands on what would be the top part of the driver's side window. At first, Joe accepts he is dead: Why else would a thing with feathers and designed for the air be on the ground? It is here to guide him to the afterworld and flutter away when it has completed its mission.

The bird bounces closer to the inside of the cab. Joe takes a closer look. He is relieved the bird is not a cardinal because he hates the St. Louis Cardinals and anything and everything associated with the team, and to be visited by said bird would be to Joe no different than the executioner insulting the condemned before the ultimate order. But the bird isn't a cardinal, any common sparrow, or a random springtime bird; it is *the* state bird. Joe sees its unique feature backlit—the rear feathers like scissors.

Now Joe begins doubting his fate of dying while on the job, and he wonders if the bird is not a guide to the afterworld but is here to lead him out of the wreckage or to lead others to him: Why else would the bird perch on the steering wheel and stare directly at Joe? Why else, Joe scrunches his face, would the bird open and close its mouth so quickly, as though it was trying to give oxygen to Joe and aid him with outliving this accident and correcting this unfortunate event; as though it has brought in its mouth some nouns and verbs that will empower him to exclaim, "I'm all right!" or "I'm in here, alive, hurry!" or "Save the art first!" to the shadows gathering outside the cab?

Joe relaxes in the seat, and everything seems to disappear; everything seems to dissolve into another realm, perhaps where it originated or where it is destined to end regardless of the number or kinds of stops along the way, including the one here this morning with the bird saying so much without speaking in a human tongue; saying something that floats to the surface in the nick of time and before a long, deep sleep.

The day is starting to turn around, the downside becoming an upside, like any good morning, the state bird waiting with him—how much better could a Wednesday rebound? Joe talks with the bird and hopes it will talk to him and keep him company and maybe tell him a story about great distances and far-off stars yet to be named. It chirps in sharp notes and hops along the dashboard and then onto his arm. Joe smiles with a few missing teeth, and he wishes he could stick his finger into the peanut butter jar lost in here and feed the weightless thing. The bird twitches its pale-gray head left to right, its eyes flashing in what little light remains in the cab. The bird flaps its wings, revealing its belly washed in pink, and starts to fly off. Joe begs it to stay, which it does and, as it returns, starts pecking Joe's hand, which speeds up time and resuscitates him more than the voices outside the cab trying to reach him, but this also annoys him and he questions why his helper has turned on him. Joe has no idea what to do, but he knows he does not want to harm the bird in any way—to do so, he fears, could bring upon him the wrath of the state and citizens brandishing torches and pitchforks; he is the bird's keeper as much as the bird has become his.

But reserves of adrenaline surge through Joe. His swats are apropos for a big man: large, meaty whacks from a smoke-colored middle-aged bear defending himself from bees after breaking open the honey hive. His forearm-heavy swings miss the bird and do nothing but agitate it and exhaust the debilitated man.

"We've got movement!" a voice yells outside the cab, which has grown darker in some corners and lighter in others with the sun closer to noon and the scissors-shaped rear of the bird flitting about like a shadow puppet.

A firefighter with a power saw cuts into the cab's door; the bird vanishes. The gap between past and present closes around Joe and nearly seals as gloves pull his legs and chest. Somebody yells his name; somebody who sounds like Dave, nearby and patting his arm, says, "We nearly lost you, but you're OK, buddy. You're OK." Joe looks around. He is in the light, moving through it on a stretcher, and he is thankful he is not heading into The Light. He sees the top of the damaged building, smoke and debris, and the accordion-crushed cab. He sees the second crane with its dinosaur neck stabilizing his crane.

Being in the open seems different to him—a rush of literal and symbolic fresh air making him aware of what he missed and, when he hears his family waits for him at the hospital, what he could have missed. The outside cracking through a stubborn pitch-black wall is what he thinks of the butterscotch light, the grass turning different shades of green, the bird, and being trapped for what felt like days but wasn't. He glances at the hoist. The artwork hovers a few inches above the roofline and appears unharmed, still packed away, still heavy on the hook when he left it, something he had hoped for but could not confirm until now.

Uptick

A late-afternoon meeting is called—atypical for 13:17 on a Wednesday but also not highly unusual because the projects each team focuses on, news, and necessary follow-ups could break at any moment during the workday. Bernstein has a good guess why the director sent the all-department email with high priority: Let's Meet – 15:00 – Conf. Rm. B. He has heard, knows well, about the rumor cocooning inside the Department of Interplanetary, Extraterrestrial, and Space Exploration nested in Building C-19. He replies to the email with an affirmative and, after clicking Send, now believes the rumor is no longer at rest but is close to molting into fact, cracking out, if it has not already cracked out, which would explain the immediacy of the meeting and why, hours before, Bowyer invited everyone in C-19 to join Team 5 for a lunchtime celebration at Bowyer's favorite downtown restaurant.

The emergency meeting would also explain why, Bernstein observed, Team 5's keyboard jockeys had, around 11:03, stopped their typing, data mining, number crunching, and caffeine consumption, in unison and eerily so, and then high-fived as dexterously as they could with their carpel-tunnel wraps snug on their wrists and hands, which, when exciting news cracked the concentrated workflow air, made them look, Bernstein has felt, having worked alongside them for years, like llamas doing the best they can to lift their legs in the air in order to click hooves.

When Bernstein rounds the corner separating his cubicle and drafting area from Team 5's cubicles and mainframes and heads toward the second floor of the facility, passing colleagues in other departments who offer hellos and good afternoons to the artist but have no idea what is emerging at his end of campus, the cheering, excitable chatter among the attendees, and clapping echo in the hallway outside Conference Room B. As soon as he enters the room, the amber afternoon sunlight shimmering on the pond carved alongside a ridge of trees handing over their summer colors, all eyes land on him, and he feels confirmed that the rumor has hatched into a thing of winged beauty and is floating around this part of the research facility; and with a grin —nearly cocky but offset with deep professional pride— notebook and pen in hand, he nods to them and takes his seat.

Handshakes, coffee mugs clinking, the remains of last week's store-bought sweets passed around, the director settles everyone down at the light-stained table in the middle of Public Relations and Information for Team 5, of which Bernstein is a long-standing, prolific, and respected member—his work featured alongside articles and as magazine inserts, on science and tech blogs, inside exhibitions, as official media releases, and as content for his wife's science-outreach projects.

After jokes about the Social Budget having enough dollar signs and decimals for today's celebration—if local, state, and federal taxpayers wouldn't mind knowing champagne, cigars, chocolates, or small gifts had been purchased—Director Lowry hands out what Team 5's lead astrophysicist and lead programmer confirmed earlier in the day. The paper slides in front of Bernstein who scans the highlights:

- 4 light years away
- Temporarily named Small Red Dot (SRD)
- About the size of Earth
- Very similar properties to Earth
- Any water that might be there would be liquid
- Orbits a red dwarf star once every two weeks
- One side of it always faces its star
- Chances of it being habitable: 26.08%

The last two bullets catch Bernstein's eyes. Bowyer and Prasad, switching between them like tag-team wrestlers, answer at first scientifically, taking the meeting on long excursions through current versus past simulations, star wobble, radioactive transference rates, and irregular versus regular orbiting habits.

But, after grumbling from PRI, the lead astrophysicist flutters his hands in the air, mumbles, struggles with grounding interstellar concepts for those who don't deal with such content on a day-to-day basis, the way Bowyer does, like a fish explaining water.

As the October sunlight lowers in the conference room and silhouettes trees, Bernstein tries his hardest not to snicker when Bowyer shifts in his seat and when a guttural noise, muffled by lively talk crisscrossing the table, rumbles from below; a foul smell follows.

The room's focus shifts to clarifying and expanding summary points. Of immediate interest is the issue of the planet being habitable. Director Lowry grabs a sesame-seed bagel and a glass of water.

"Should I should make the planet look like the next place where humans could visit and, possibly, make a home?" Bernstein asks before Bowyer excuses himself from the meeting and Prasad takes over. Bernstein has a good guess why the lead astrophysicist vacates his chair.

"There's much more to consider," Prasad emphasizes. "Team 5 is at least ten years out from working with respective teams. Propulsion and Fuels. Robotics. Optics. On-site Advancement. And sending probes with sensors and cameras."

Bernstein nods to Prasad, who with his youthful, buoyant charm, his round glasses, and his calm voice, explains what such a place may look like to humans. His tone and volume, Bernstein has noted, having collaborated with him on preliminary sketches of an asteroid impacting a moon, which Prasad said they were "poetically truthful," are qualities someone would want to hear while storm clouds engulf a sunny day.

Returning to the second-from-bottom bullet, Bernstein asks, "What does it specifically mean? And how does it tether to what the scientists want to see in a conceptual drawing?"

"Because one side always faces the sun," Prasad answers in delight. "The newly discovered planet's sky would include an unforgettable surface and sky. But technical details aren't enough. You should provide an into-the-marrow response. I'm not opposed to calling it SRD for the time being."

Bernstein reclines in his chair and makes a few notes.

"You will need to craft a powerful official release for the general public," Prasad continues. He washes down a sprinkle donut with hot tea. "The image must surpass the words. He chuckles. "Everyone on social media will love to hashtag 'Small Red Dot.'"

Everyone from PRI, including Bernstein, chuckle along.

"The planet's color may be the most important factor in presenting Team 5's finding. The color would be familiar to the world. *Our* world." Prasad smiles. "A color so recognizable and intimate and found everywhere on Earth, no matter the season. A color that may have different names in different languages but is as primal as the need to move toward it."

Bowyer, pale faced and sweaty, adjusts his seat. Tasks and due dates are assigned; Director Lowry trusts each department manager will maintain check-ins and production schedules. They all agree on a release date: the first Tuesday of November, three weeks from today. The meeting adjourns.

Back in his cubicle, Bernstein scribbles for a few minutes and draws a canyon with a single bright star over it. He stops when Jacob texts—he is home from school, homework done—followed by a text from Joan who is ready to be picked up at Building E-17 Annex 2, which is Education and Outreach's storage warehouse stuffed with props, displays, and learning materials for schools, planetariums, museums, and fairs. He stares at the sunset and can't decide if its blood-like crimson pulls off or seeps into the blue.

That night after dinner, Bernstein and his son sit on the living room couch. He tells Jacob, "It's a new project I can't say anything about until it's public."

Joan kicks out the chair's footrest and clicks off the TV before opening her book. "I know what it is," she sings, teasing Jacob.

"Come on! That's not fair!"

Winking at Joan, Bernstein leans to Jacob. "It has something to do with a planet, and I'll interpret what scientists inferred happened long ago and far away from Earth. We had a meeting about it all." He wipes his eyes from laughing. "One of us in there was having a marathon."

Confusion squishes Jacob's face.

"A string of SBDs." Bernstein's lips motor out flatulent sounds. "That conference room was so smelly, but we had to sit there because of something important and amazing."

The two of them giggle, snort, elbow ribs.

"What are you two up to?" Joan asks, wrinkling her nose at them.

"It's Dad, I swear."

The clock chimes half past eight.

"Goodnight." Jacob kisses them. "I'll see you bright and early tomorrow."

"Yes, you will. We love you."

After Jacob heads to bed, Bernstein laughs again.

"What?"

"Whenever Bowyer goes out for lunch at Taqueria Azteca, he never strays from ordering his usual. And the outcome is the same. El Grande Burrito with Salsa del Diablo. It's delivered in a black bottle with a skull-shaped stopper. The Lord of Darkness on the front label has a basket of tortilla chips." He sighs and shows her his quick sketches and color tests.

She taps one. "If this is approved, I want to use it for upcoming events. I'd love to incorporate the final version with the latest news." She holds it up like a piece of stained glass and tells him it's about the future. The color is a reason for rising every morning.

• • •

Row by row the overhead lights clank off, and the horseshoe-shaped theater is nearly dark, save for the red light swirling on the chrome structures outlining a spaceship's bridge. A portable laboratory, computers, and three-dimensional models of the Solar System sit on a long metal table at the stage's opposite end. Celestial blues and explosive oranges, images of stars and galaxies whiz by on the large screen next to the one door on stage; dry ice fumes underneath. The kids are restless while their parents snicker, blush, and shake their heads at music blasting from the corner speakers and at the lyrics adjusted from saucy to nerdy.

The regional buyer for The Nature Store in the Springdale Mall chuckles, having grooved to the song as a teenager, cruised the mall's food court and its department stores, or took long, slow drives up and down streets in summer, windows down, warm air pouring in, when Debbie promised to her friends and herself that, after high school, she would never return to Springdale again. "Let's talk about space, ba-by/Let's talk about you and me/Let's talk about inter-dimensional theories that may be/Let's talk about space."

As she sits with the kids oblivious to the parodied lyrics but bobbing up and down, she reminds herself that being alone and being lonely are different, life's grays having doubled and flooded, and that since high school her way out hasn't disappeared as much as it has rerouted her to a world of spreadsheets, price points, and inventories of animals; CDs of whale recordings and rainforest sounds; and telescopes, planispheres, and brain games in a store not making enough money on a daily basis owned by a company lost underneath online shopping.

A nebula pans across the screen, the red light stops swirling, and the loud robotic voiceover on the speakers kills the song. "Are YOU ready for soooooome SCI-ENCE?" The last syllables of *science* disintegrate into a digitized echo. The crowd claps and whistles. Dr. Simon's Super-Sized Super-Fun Space-Time-Continuum Science Show starts a few minutes behind the morning schedule.

Donning a lab coat, hair disheveled, Dr. Simon bursts from the door and slides from the vapors with his tall, ramen noodle–thin body. "Wad up, Exploratorium Science Fall Days?" he yells into the headset's microphone after scanning the back row where a young woman standing there sets down her whiteboard, wipes off said venue, and moves behind the stage, flicking a switch as she does.

The red light over the chrome frame of the spaceship bridge–laboratory swirls again and belts a warning note. Kids cover their ears. One little girl mouths *Too loud* to her mom who agrees. The modified hip-hop classic kicks in again, lasers gyrate over the stage, and Dr. Simon shimmies his rear end, accented by zigzagging blue and green beams. The kids can't stop jiggling, and Debbie can't stop watching.

"Have we got a great show for you today. It's going to be…" Dramatic pause. "Out of this world!" Dr. Simon throws his arms toward the giant screen upon which a satellite image of the Hall of Science and Engineering roof shrinks, the fairgrounds shrink (the buildings and the acres like latticework), the town of Springdale shrinks, Jefferson County shrinks, the state shrinks (thinning blues of rivers and lakes), the region rolls from greens to clouds, the country shrinks, the continent, the planet.

Yes! two boys pump their arms; one of them stands up and hoola-hoops in front of his seat. A few girls cover their mouths when Earth is a pale blue dot. One girl with beads in her braids raises her hand.

"Questions after the show," Dr. Simon says.

"But…"

"Questions after the show," the assistant repeats.

"But the speed of…"

"Let's get to it." Dr. Simon spins toward the control panel blinking by the large screen and downshifts a lever while spinning a wheel.

Off they go toward the inner planets, starting with an orbit around the Sun. As they leave light and heat, traveling through a looping solar flame, silence consumes the theater.

Dr. Simon asks, "Which planet is next?"

Debbie knows, having grown familiar with games, books, and toys at the shop, and she wants to yell it out. Crazy single woman showing up grade schoolers…and a major demographic at the store, she thinks. Yet another victory notch for adult me.

The little boy with a mole on his chin who leapfrogged onto stage when the assistant selected him looks like a deer in headlights. The other kids bite their lips, grimace, and latch onto their hair, while Jordan twists his shoulders back and forth on stage, tugs at his crotch, and scans the seats for his parents in the fourth row who may have a hint or the correct answer for him. Mom shakes her head no at the pizzicato technique of his pants grabbing and then smiles; Dad nods *Go on, buddy* with his chin's genetically matching mole. Jordan sucks in his face, bugs his eyes, and blurts out an answer that brings the pain of defeat and shame to his little colleagues who, out of respect for Jordan's tiny window of concentration, supported him in silence.

Debbie muffles her laugh.

The show must go on, and the assistant clips a participation ribbon onto Jordan and sends him back to the seats.

Dr. Simon takes them past Mercury.

Mercury, Jordan. Mercury, Debbie thinks. Not I Don't Know with the moons I Guess and Shoulder Shrug.

The ship hovers in front of the planet second from the Sun. "Which is?"

Debbie also knows this as tiny arms shoot up around her. Some of the kids bypass general communal politeness—Jordan's previous humiliating loss fresh in their minds—and shout out "Venus!" Dr. Simon confirms and adds that it was named after, his voice lowering to the deep-bass end of the scale, the Greek goddess of *luh-uv*. He winks at the audience, receiving giggles from some kids, gagging from some of the boys, eye rolling from some moms, blushing from others, and yawns from the dads, most of whom have started scrolling through their phones.

The ship completes its tour of the Solar System. "And now, let's leave our neck of the woods and head *waaaay* to the edge of our solar system. Four light-years away, where we think this planet could hold water…and life."

The audience oohs and ahhs when Dr. Simon steers the ship down into the atmosphere and over rocks, craters, and valleys. All eyes squint at the screen for signs of life. The land is not alien to Debbie; it reminds her of a summer trip her family took, when she was a child, to the scrubbed blacks and volcanic hues of New Mexico mesas. Seeing the planet's vast openness, she jokes to herself one side of the political aisle would refuse believing forms of life exist on another planet and Big Money would capitalize on this planet's resources, driving up real estate and costs of living, but the other side of the political aisle would protect the planet, as well as all the diverse life that is and is not yet known, with so many laws and fines that everything would have to ask for permission to live by volition. The sky's color overwhelms the audience and her. She has seen such a sky before and wants it for the store as much as for herself.

After the show, Debbie makes her way backstage where Dr. Simon, drenched in sweat, chugs a bottle of blue Gatorade. She asks the young woman playing the assistant, "Are you Joan Bernstein?"

"She's over there."

Debbie walks to the middle the middle-aged woman cradling a phone and typing on a laptop, her shirt stitched with SPRINGDALE NATIONAL RESEARCH FACILITY – EDUCATION AND OUTREACH. "Ms. Bernstein, I'm Debbie Getty, the buyer for The Nature Store for this region. We talked the other day about maybe getting some educational and promotional materials at the store from you."

"Oh yes. Nice to meet you in person. Please call me Joan."

"Great show."

"Thank you."

"Do you have time to talk now?"

"Give me one sec." After finishing her call, Joan grabs two chairs near big metal boxes and storage bins and motions to the rear bumper of the U-Haul truck emptied of the show's contents.

"That planet was something."

"Right? My husband and his team did all that."

"It was so far away from us, strange…and yet so familiar."

The two women talk business options, financial numbers, inventory availability, logistics, appropriate school-grade levels. The show's assistant interrupts, saying she and Greg are headed out for coffee and to grab some duct tape, wires, and chrome polish. The two women agree to general terms and a request for proposal.

"Do you think we can dream there?" Debbie asks.

"Where?" Joan replies, closing her laptop and sliding it into a briefcase.

"The planet we ended at."

Joan stares at the serious face across from her and waits for a few seconds before answering. "I don't think there's anything in the universe that says we can't." She slings the briefcase over her shoulder. On the bag's front is the phrase LOVE YOU TO THE MOON AND BACK scribbled like child handwriting in a spectrum of crayons. "We need to get some supplies before the next show. In the meantime, let me give you some test samples." She walks over to the truck. "You can see how they do in your store, and we can go from there." She hands a thick package to Debbie.

"I can't wait to see what's in here."

"A lot of the content from today's show, in various media. Posters, puzzles, DVDs."

"Thank you. I'll be in touch."

The two women shake hands.

Blink your eyes and the world is a different color, Debbie thinks and spins around, but Joan has vanished, as have the assistant and the man playing Dr. Simon. She looks at the backstage mechanics, at the stage, bristling with electricity, and sealed between, at the curtain illustrated with planets, comets, and constellations. The sky has not let go, and it has uncovered her desires section by section, opened like the doors on an Advent calendar. Her heart could be shaped like anything other than a tight fist: a robin sleeping in a nest, a piece of glass, a light bulb, a red seed. If only…, she thinks. All this could be possible on a ship fired like a bullet from a gun brought into a field endlessly filled with stars.

• • •

Panic rushing her. Panic grabbing her when she looked away—seconds, she replays in her head—when she stood next to him, holding his hand and hoping he would love this or that, whatever it was she could buy for him, wrap it in ribbons, and place it under the tree. Maybe from Santa; maybe from the two of them. Panic when she stormed into the security office after wrestling the doorknob, her hands tightening and unable to grip anything in front of her, including details she cannot hold, minutes she has lost. Panic increasing, the doorknob not turning, she smacked her palms on the window, like a body slapping water, which caused Officer Wooten to fling the door open and see her sweating, pale, a ghost searching for a ghost, her hands arthritic from clutching at nothing, the day emptied, Black Friday blacker, her arms weighed down by shopping bags, so much weight she is carrying and holding on a doorstep, Laurie pleading, sobbing. He was next to me. He was next to me. Her words like a hymn lamented in the wind. This panic gnawing as she stumbles behind Officer Wooten's question he repeats, bringing her back to the question for which she has no clear answer. Where? he asks. Take some breaths and tell me where you last were. He sets down a cup of water and a box of tissues in front of her. She can't drink, can't clutch. Ma'am, where did you last see him? I don't know. She stares at Officer Wooten's square face and is as lost to him as her son is to her.

A desk calendar has the upcoming weeks highlighted in yellow; the word UPTICK written in red ink over the days' boxes. What does your son look like? This high—Laurie holds her hand to the side of her leg as she paces across the carpet. Sam, she clears her throat, Samuel Keene. Blue jacket, gloves, and a scarf in his jacket's pockets. Jacket has a hood lined with white fabric. Bright red sneakers. Dark hair, dark eyes. Korean, she gasps like a confession, which has, every now and then, garnered double takes from those people looking at the petite, natural blonde, honeycomb dripping in a jar, her blue eyes bluer now from sobbing. Office Wooten keeps writing; no pause-and-stare. Laurie manages to sit. Sam can't hear too well in either ear—the right's tympanum damaged from his birth mother's complicated pregnancy; his left ear deformed like a pumpkin dropped on the ground. Not deaf, she emphasizes—hearing impaired. He only knows a few words when reading lips or when you're close to him. But he is, she chimes, the sweetest boy you'll ever meet, loving and kind, and he can't wait for Christmas partly because of the presents, yes, but partly because he can't wait for *Messiah* at their church, as the three of them sang with the congregation last year, holding each other in the middle of the pew.

Officer Wooten says this happens more than you think this time of year and most of the time the kids are so close by it all turns out all right. Laurie wonders what most of the time means. Better than half? I don't have the numbers, but I'd say it's close to a ninety-percent success rate. At least a ten percent chance something else, something tragic and horrific could happen scuttles in her head. She has seen the news and now she feels she is one of those parents, one of them, her photo promulgated on the Internet as an example of why people like her shouldn't adopt, proving this would work out under normal circumstances. Does he have a favorite place here he may go to? He likes skateboards and the calendars in those small gazebos by the fountains—you know, bright, loud things—but I can't think of anything right now. It's OK, ma'am. We've only been here when it's not like this, she says, and we don't usually come this time of year because of all this. The office walls barely muffle the chaos outside. Take your time, ma'am. She knows he's wrong when he offers this. Taking time to think is taking time away from finding him.

Sam will show up unscathed. He's probably still on the premises. Officer Wooten is certain. He puts out a Missing Child Alert to his fellow security personnel. Most of the time they will tell someone they are lost, or someone will figure out they are lost and will notify a store manager or us here at security. We can canvas the area. He offers to refill her water before they leave. Most of the time, Laurie echoes to herself. How many other officers do you have? Five. Five, she gasps, for a day like today? Officer Wooten holsters his radio and grabs his jacket. Ten legs and boots searching over one million square feet congested with crowds, sounds, and sales. She sinks inside herself. Five officers from TaskForce Security Inc. will not find her son.

They begin on the first floor, near the frozen yogurt shop and inside the aromas of coffee and freshly baked cinnamon rolls. Simply retrace your steps. Officer Wooten remains upbeat. Laurie splits the crowd down the middle, hunting down time and the trail it leaves behind. She hasn't and won't text Karen. How quickly this happened; how quickly this can end. She wanders among the people, places, and things that have consumed her child. He could be in any number of stores, behind any number of glass windows—the repetition of products and special prices clogging sightlines. How many boys look like him? Same clothes, same height. So much blending in the architecture of her memory. Have you seen my son? Heads shake, phones pop out, condolences, prayers, good lucks. Strangers hug her or rub her arms; most offer to help.

Sam! she screams by the indoor playground with its dinosaur slide, cave, and giant bones. Sam Keene! Ma'am, ma'am, please. Officer Wooten catches up to her. We don't need to do that. People stare as they walk by. Maybe, she hopes, he has told someone who looks trusting and, if looks aren't deceiving, will take him to the security office or to one of the stores. Maybe someone will notice this young boy is by himself; this Good Samaritan will help him, asking Sam if he's lost. Laurie looks at Officer's Wooten radio silent by his side.

There! Laurie points. That shop! We were there last. She runs toward the display with its red and green lights and silver tinsel. He had been next to her while she admired the sweater's pattern. She looked at the sale price and wished she and Karen could afford it, if not for Sam's medical expenses. She had wondered if her favorite necklace would snag on the delicate braided fabric—hand-made in small batches, the sign advertised, and from sheep born and bred in the Scotland—perhaps tearing the sweater apart like clouds every time she took off the heirloom her grandfather gave to her grandmother who gave it as a blessing on the eve of Laurie and Karen's wedding—the feather-shaped pendant inscribed with one line from her grandmother's favorite poem about hope. Standing there, minutes before Sam vanished, Laurie had texted Karen and asked her if she wanted anything on sale. Save it, she replied. Get him whatever he wants within reason :), the two of them steering the seven-year-old away from materialism, focusing on the other spirit of the season, mindful of not spoiling him on his first Christmas with them—no more foster parents, no more pieces moved into place before pulled away.

Staring into the store from the display window, Laurie watches Officer Wooten talk to the manager, who picks up a phone, hangs up after a few minutes, and walks over to the employees working behind the counter and the customers snaking on the floor. Several of them look up; some don't stop folding clothes or checking sizes. The manager shakes her head no and glances between the mannequin and the snowflake-shaped sale sign.

Officer Wooten returns. He suggests heading over to the skateboard shop and then to the fountains where the nearby kiosks sell those calendars she had mentioned. Laurie breaks away from him, shoves her way up the escalator toward the second floor, and sprints into the place that has captivated Sam when they come to the Springdale Mall.

She finds him at the back of the store standing mesmerized in front of a large television screen rolling through the latest science and nature news, her son with a gourd-shaped ear, not hearing his name called, but she calls it anyway. She touches his shoulder, but he doesn't face her. The program's voiceover describes the newly discovered planet as the best of all possibilities for life. He moves closer to the canyons and the crimson-purple light spreading behind ridges of rocks and glazes of clouds and the sky saturated with the color of a perpetual sunset.

Start of the Season

Something about a tattoo he had and wanted to talk to her about while they stayed on the cape. Not wanting to make a big deal about it, but he wanted her to know. From his youth, he said, smiling when he mentioned this feature, which she had not yet seen, somewhere on his body, Tom mentioning this as casually as someone saying clouds were starting to roll in on the horizon. Around the thirtieth minute into the excursion he brought it up—between the middle of the ocean, with its sunset-laced waves, and the dock where they boarded with their luggage and fellow hotel guests, this point of departure that had sunk in the distance with the oncoming night.

He didn't offer anything else and returned to watching the ocean landscape roll past them in reds and pinks underneath descending bands of blue-black. Strings of lights brightened here and there in front of them as the boat neared the resort's dock, which was well lit with large lamps and staff wearing reflective vests and holding glowing batons. Sheila didn't ask for anything else, smiled with a reply of "Sure, of course," and remained close to Tom, their fingers interlocked, as he leaned on the guardrail.

But she couldn't help weigh the timing of his revelation and hesitation to open it further until later during their first get-away together as a couple.

The water, sun, and wind ensconced them as the boat's speakers squawked when one of the crew reminded everyone, near dusk, to keep their eyes open for bottlenose dolphins playing in the engine's wake. Tom pointed out several of them popping up and down, like ink squirting through water, trying to keep up with the boat's speed, and showing off. "They know we're watching this late," he said. Sheila laughed with him and tried finding an image, a symbol, or one word or a string of words inside his dress shirt, at the base of his neck, or parts of his arms she had, for some reason, never noticed before. She squinted at the white fabric, assuming something heavily inked, if it was heavily inked, would emerge like colors through fog.

The late-evening sun silhouetted the island and the blocks of hotel properties. In one of those blocks, one of those buildings would be theirs for the next week. A room with a view of paradise—the online description pitched—perfect for lovers old and young, first time or long time. The crowd gathered by the boat's railing, and Sheila struggled remembering which property —perhaps the one with colonial Spanish features and its red-tile roof and arcades; perhaps the tropical one with palm trees stair-casing up toward the lobby entrance; perhaps the ultra-sleek, modern one with its onyx-like glass that, hours ago, had reflected the bright day and now reflected the end-of-day spectrum. She hoped to see animals—baby goats, donkeys, beach-combing horses—and flora and fauna bursting in the area, but she couldn't remember which room or which property, shining in the dark, awaited them. Tom's tattoo was all she could think about.

With a few blasts on the horn acknowledging its arrival, the boat rocked into the dock. The gangplank lowered; a thin line of passengers wearing backpacks or carrying few items disembarked first. Tom kissed her on the cheek before departing for the space where they had stowed their bags. The sun was low enough that its cooling residue slid across the ocean's surface. Shelia could see the outlines of the buildings, but this time, they were more pronounced and more developed than when they were far away; patches of darkness filled areas of the property where footlights, the cabanas, and the rooms' lights fell short. *Listen, while we're here*—his opening words echoed in her head.

She helped Tom with their bags, and as he did before they boarded the boat, he commented on how beautiful she looked in her dress with its lime-green accents in the shapes of flowers scattered over a white background, her skin contrasting with the latter. She had ditched the broad-brimmed hat after sunset. Her hat reminded him of Derby Day—an adventure they should take this coming May because it was something all good Kentuckians should do in their lives. She had blushed then and, now, clipped the hat to her suitcase by the brown ribbon matching her eyes.

Tom wiped remaining sunscreen off his upper lip before he kissed her and they walked with some of their fellow travelers toward the hotel.

She didn't know what else to make of his on-the-way-here comment. She hadn't been on an excursion like this one—with anyone, ever, and certainly not anyone like Tom who had drawn her in and, he had told her, she to him. The trips she had been on were work-related, rambled up and down the mid-Atlantic states—D.C. her northernmost point, Miami her southernmost—and required her to be professionally dressed, exact, and never fumble over her presentations or the materials she pitched; money, culture, and history were at stake. She watched his pace as they passed an open-pit BBQ. Smells of coconut and grilled fish and chicken wafted, drinks clinking and people cavorting—all of this unfolding in soft light and the moon starting to appear. Tom's pace was precise and direct—wanting to reach an endpoint, and he wanted to reach it without stopping.

When he is ready, she told herself and entered the lobby through the large wooden doors and crossed the terra-cotta tile floor upon which rested the main desk where the maître d' signed them in.

• • •

In the fall, the museum had started ramping up efforts to promote an exhibition opening in January about African-American abstract painters and modernism. Sheila was that field's curator and expert; the exhibition—its research and organization—was a massive achievement as well as a personal and professional goal for her.

One of the marketing assistants suggested hiring a jazz band for the show's Friday night opening; she knew a band from one of the well-established, classy restaurants in Louisville. Tom was part of the band—the drummer with a knack for timing, individual flair when it was needed, and soft touches on the slow ballads bringing couples dancing at the front of the stage after their dinners had settled, some drinks had kicked in, and connections electrified the night air.

Sheila and the marketing assistant went to check out the band. Tom and Sheila made eye contact right away. His flattened face could have been a boxer's or a wrestler's; his left earlobe dropped lower than his right; his pale blue eyes were square, save for the ends curling down like fine fishing line toward his uneven cheeks. He had full lips, as though their swelling never receded; the top lip's scar zigzagged up toward the bottom of his nose; and he spoke with a slight stutter Sheila could tell came on when he was nervous—but it did not when he stood next to her.

He introduced himself after the first half, and after the full set was over, he sat with her and had one beer and then water; she kept to red wine and stopped after a few glasses and shared his water. She said she was Methodist; he said he was Catholic, new to it, having been confirmed not too long ago, learning and growing, which was the opposite of what he was back in his twenties and teens. Not agnostic, he said. *A nihilist* were the words he used. "Nothing at all," he admitted and shook the hands of some patrons on their way out. The athletic tape wrapped around the fleshy parts of this thumbs had loosened from sweat and playing. He had rough hands and palms as though they had been dragged over rocks and dried in chalk; he rubbed them together as he sat near the door letting in cool night air every time it opened.

They talked about music. His first love had been country and old-timey folk songs; he had found and fell for other styles and genres. She wanted to know how he became part of the group. "Friend of a friend," he said, mentioning that Rachel, one of the flautists from the Philharmonic, used to play in a jazz band that often shared the stage with his band but had no more time for it because of tutoring and recording an album. She knew he was interested in all kinds of music, wanted to challenge his chops, and wouldn't mind an extra gig or two on the side. He told Sheila he was excited to play that style of music, having listened to it like it was once contraband, and loved every minute of the band's ribbing him in a good-hearted way until he was a member.

"Part-time," he said. "I still got my day job at the Phil. Speaking of…we should swap."

She beamed at him.

"You show me the museum, and I'll show you practice in the Big Hall…that's what we call it. Plus, I'd like to know you a little more. I'd like to see you again." He helped her with her coat and contacted her the next day.

At the museum, he wandered the galleries and stopped when something caught his eyes or when she pointed out certain things, highlights of the collection, or items on loan.

"On loan," he teased.

"That's right."

"Swap."

"Swap," she echoed, laughing with him.

"I wasn't good at this kind of stuff, but I like it. I like someone showing it to me." He bent at the waist to look closer at a painting. His left hip jutted like a rock as he did, and he was slow to pick himself up and continue on, grimacing as though he needed a cane. He noticed the brush strokes or lack thereof— sometimes only stains and palette-knife sculpting and scraping; the energy thrown into the paint—the whole body and mind at work; and tension between the messages of the artists as they lived in one world and created in another but never, he understood, leaving one for the other—or that they were ever fully able to or welcomed in. "I get that," he said to her.

At the rehearsal she attended, he wasn't where he said he would be. She looked around and couldn't find him. He eventually emerged from the back in a starched dress shirt and walked to the percussion pit. They saw each other, and he bobbed his head toward her as she sat in the shadows of the seats facing the middle of the stage. He saw her smile; she shook her head and, as discretely as she could, pointed *Pay attention, you!*

The conductor picked up his baton, looked over the players, and motioned *And one, two.* On his third tap, flutes, oboes, and violins flurried through the air like stars succeeding one another. Tom's march-like accents on the timpani deepened these sounds and accompanied the choir's verse of the first cantata.

Afterward, he said to Sheila that the opening bars made him feel as though the notes circled around him like points on a celestial globe. The sounds ran across his jaw and found a way inside to buoy him—this sensation never failed to emerge no matter how many times they had practiced, no matter what notes he knew lay ahead. He slid his drumsticks into a bag, said goodnight to his colleagues, walked her to her car, and kissed her for the first time.

They went on more dates. Most of the leaves on the trees had reached their autumn peak, and some had started dropping. The sky was cloudless blue; the air was crisp. They hiked; they found local eateries that had avoided hype; they visited the distilleries; they talked on the phone and in person until he joked he was too tired to play because of all their talking, which was OK by him because, if the Phil were to fire him or the E Tones were to kick him out, he could spend more time with her. He told her they were turning into a typical Boy Meets Girl story—head over heels, smitten from day one; their time together was building into something he could not deny or let go. He told her he loved her and he meant that—not a thing he would say to get her into bed or something out of desperation—but he truly loved her, and if she didn't love him or couldn't return love in any capacity other than friendship, he would be OK with that; he would love her no matter what she chose.

She told him she was growing to love him. They had only kissed, held hands, snuggled on couches, watched movies in bed; they took their time with it all and waited until an anniversary of some sort arrived, and when it did, he thought they should find some time to get away and celebrate. The Phil had a short break after Thanksgiving and before final rehearsals for the Holiday show. She could use a break from prepping for her show, and her calendar would allow her to sneak off for at least five days, and upon returning, she would have to crank up effort for the last leg.

"It would be worth it," he said. He would meet her family before Christmas and she would meet his after New Year's; hers would sit in the best seats he could get for them at the *Oratorio* and they could watch him play; she would reserve tickets for the first Saturday afternoon his parents were free. But before any potential family drama or holiday stress, they decided to get away —just the two of them. Baja, he suggested—whales migrating south this time of year, the start of the season for them. She loved the destination and the reason and that she would be with him, these promises he made in an amount of time that was theirs; these promises, he pointed out, made indoors—he and Sheila being with each other indoors more times than not; that they should be outdoors and outside of what they had and what they knew.

· · ·

They walked into the room, and as they placed their toiletries on the stone counter, the reasons why she and Tom had picked it together that night they spent in front of her laptop looking over search results, prices, and amenities rushed back to her—the bright tile, the spa tub, the timber beams plastered into the ceiling, the adobe walls, the back patio with a view of the ocean, and the skylight framing the night sky. Room service had left mints and chocolates on a silver tray and, on the wooden bathroom door, had hung two bathrobes smelling like lavender. A bottle of champagne on ice and two glasses with ribbons wrapped around the stems (Tom and Sheila's names printed on the ribbons) waited on a nightstand.

She suggested strolling along the beach before dinner; the extra hours they gained flying west had energized her in one way, but feeling low on food and water, she also wanted to eat. She grabbed a sweater from the suitcase and opened a water bottle from the fridge.

Tom agreed, but before they stepped out, he wanted to talk to her about what he mentioned on the way here—now, if she didn't mind because it was important to him. "To us," he added.

She placed the sweater over her lap, folded her hands, and waited. He sat next to her on the bed; his posture curved like a question mark. Less than two hours had passed since the boat ride, and it felt much longer to her. The sun had fully set; scraps of moonlight lay across parts of the beach and slivers of it inside the ocean. Part of her wanted to save talking for the morning.

His eyes flickered between her face and the ocean rolling onto the beach in the distance behind them. "So, this tattoo I have," he said, unbuttoning his dress shirt. His hands shook. One arm pulled itself from a sleeve, the other shortly behind, and he moved as though chronic injuries plagued his shoulders. Both arms out stood in the room's soft amber light. No visible tattoo.

She had never seen him shirtless before. One of these nights during their getaway she knew she would see and be with him in a different way—but she did not anticipate seeing or being with him this way.

He peeled off his t-shirt. Nothing on his chest or stomach or shoulders, save for blemishes. His jaw tensed as he grimaced; his tongue stuck between his teeth as though he tasted something sticky and invisible in the air making him unable to answer and making movement and memory his only words, if not an imperfect answer, for her. He put both hands on his knees after he adjusted his feet, slid his hips over the blanket, and pivoted toward her as much as his body could.

The tattoo wasn't large; it covered one hand-width of his middle back; and it looked like it could have been bigger, more aggressive, but it had been stopped. It looked like propeller blades frozen in their rotation and had once been red, white, and black. A section of his spine stuck out slightly below the tattoo's center point and enhanced his body's imperfections and the tattoo's impermanence; he had little fat or muscle there, akin to someone having once wasted away or having shouldered something for a long time.

The colors had faded and one-third of the outline had been erased until the skin it once held looked like peeled sunburn. She knew the symbol immediately and what it and others like it stood for, and it divided her from him until she felt she was in another time and another place but that she was the same person who now had to face a gap between what she had hoped and experienced as hope and a past that could eclipse hope.

She knew the image on his back, more than halfway up, near the scarred plane of skin between his shoulder blades and base of his neck, was no longer what she had wondered about on the boat ride and returned to during their time on land, a worry she wanted to dismiss quickly—and did, but could not stop recurring—because of the fear and deceit it had pulled from obscurity. But there now on his back was no longer a general worry for her to place on a general image but a specific image piercing her with precision without him having to say anything as the day settled.

"You were part of this?" she asked him. And before he could answer, she continued, "You must have been. Why else would you have it?"

"I was. Yes. For a couple of years." His lips trembled. "Twenty-five years ago. I was a stupid seventeen-year-old and a different person, and I'm not that anymore. I wasn't ever really. I mean…wasn't that way. I didn't know what I was doing at that age. I needed something to belong to, and that's all that I had at the time."

"The things we all know and read about…they did them…my grandparents, their parents, families *they* knew. They still do things."

"I know."

"We are all part of that…and you're part of it."

"No."

"Yes…in a way, yes, with *that*." Her eyes flickered toward his back as though they wanted to see a ghost but not linger where it loomed.

"That wasn't me…and it's *not* me. It may have been but not anymore. I got out…all of it. I had no education to speak of. I had nothing before I was in and nothing when I got out. But I had music. I understood. I got out. Those auditions were the most important things…until now." He wrapped his t-shirt into a ball and wiped his eyes. "I just wanted you to know."

She rolled in her lips; seconds passed before she spoke again. "I believe that you're out. I believe you're not that person anymore. But…"

"I know." He inhaled and exhaled deeply. "When I'm done at the gym, I don't change shirts. I can't. There are showers there, but no way. No way. So, then I go to practice because I can't go home to change because of traffic and driving back to the other side of town. But I get to this place where I am accepted for what I can do and for who I am *now*, but I can't change clothes there. I have to wait for every guy in there to leave or do something else while I change. So there I am, waiting as long as possible…drinking more and more coffee, watching the little TV that we have, messing around on my phone, making small talk. Do you think I want to be on my phone that much or talk about whatever?" He rubbed excess sweat from his hands into his pants. "Bruce, one of the trumpets, teased me about doing double duty and being a liaison for our social media. A live, real-time feed. 'Live from the pit,' he said. It's all in fun, I know, but… I change in a bathroom stall when no one watches. I walk out with a clean t-shirt on and a sweaty gym shirt in my hand. Either no one notices or no one cares. I finish getting ready, and I'm always the last one to practice."

"This wasn't a thing you got for initiation, for doing something. Is it?"

"No."

"You didn't do anything to anyone…ever?"

"No."

"Never laid hands on anybody."

"No."

"What did you do?"

"Had meetings. Talked about whatever they were angry about. That's it. A lot of talk. Flags and signs and…horrible music." He forced a smile. "It was all talk. Nothing more, nothing less. And…yes…I said things at the time…with them…the typical things. I regret that…all of it." He again wiped his hands on his pants. "I'm done with it. I have been for a long while. I got out before I got in too deep. They didn't like it when I left. But they're a long ways away now."

She looked at his face when he said this—its contours and disproportions; the imbalances and the scars carved across his body.

"I'd be covered in ink if I hadn't. I'd be making this dermatologist I've been going to a whole lot richer."

She smiles at him.

"I love you," he said. "I didn't want to keep it from you. Besides, how was I going to?" He motioned his hand throughout the room and slipped on his t-shirt. "I understand if you want to stop…what we have. I understand if you tell someone…your sister or brother or friends, and this could stop. But I don't want it to."

She nodded, kissed him on his forehead, and suggested they skip the restaurant and order in; the restaurant and its celebrated chef would still be there tomorrow and for the rest of their time here. "I'll have to wait for that flan later," she said, breaking another build-up of silence and smiling with him as he pushed off the bed, grabbed the remote, and dialed room service.

The large flat-screen TV clicked on to the peninsula's promotional channel. Activities brightened in front of them. He offered a glass of champagne, which she took and clinked his glass. He flopped down next to her, and they started talking about all that they would do—that there was much to do; that the images and the happy faces on the screen had unlimited access to joys. Within the first few hours of being here, they joked they hadn't been anywhere else or done anything but unpack and talk in the room.

To hold her over until room service arrived, he offered one of the chocolates and a napkin from the silver tray between them on the bed, and she remembered one of their earlier dates at the restaurant overlooking the river. He had glanced around after he uncapped an ink pen he had inside his blazer. She watched him draw on the back of the copy of the check; he slid it toward her.

"I get this weekly email from this self-improvement-making-better-decisions website, and this one talked about choice and responsibility. And, I bet you know it. I never did until the other day. Maybe you came across it in college. The guy who wrote it said it's popular in ethics classes."

He had drawn a set of train tracks cutting right to left across the back of the check, and at the end, the tracks crumbled from a cliff. A set of tracks branched off from this main set and wound their way to the top at a Stop sign he colored in. Off to the side of this branch, he had drawn a stick figure and, after looking at Sheila while he drew, added a dress and her hair, earrings, and glasses. She rolled her eyes at him while looking over the rim of her drink. The stick figure held a switch bolted into the imaginary ground. A different stick figure stood on the tracks leading to the Stop sign. A trolley rambled one quarter of the way over the main tracks.

"So, this trolley has lost its brakes, and it can continue its current path." He pointed to the tracks falling off the cliff's edge. "And everyone aboard will die, but you don't know any of the passengers." He tapped the stick figure wearing the dress. "Or, if you pull the switch, it will stop safely up here but will kill the one person you know best and love." He tapped the stick figure on the tracks leading to the Stop sign. "Do you intervene? The many over the one, or the one over the many? But here's a kicker. The writer said, 'What if no one but you and whoever you pick are the only ones to know about this? No one else knows or will ever find out. Does that make a difference in your choice now?'"

Room service knocked on the door and wheeled in their food—salmon and wild rice for him, chicken tamales for her wrapped, the menu said, *in husks from corn grown in our garden.* As Tom served her, they resumed talking about what they would see on their outings. Probably a stunning sunrise. Eat authentic huevos rancheros. Drink real Mexican coffee—not the imported-frozen-and-transported kind they bought at grocery stores. Of all his promises, getting to the cape and getting off it in order to explore the ocean was the one she wanted him to keep. They talked about whale watching on Wednesday, as scheduled, another promise he would like for them to keep—another thing outside and in the daylight.

They finished eating, had a few more chocolates and emptied the champagne, held each other in bed, and returned to the whales: gray whales rolling their backs, coming up for air, pursuing a path south toward warmer water—through which the cape rose, on top of which the hotel was built, inside of which the bodies in the room floated on this warmer water and shelf of hard rock and soft coastlines; the whales floating in their motion; the ocean moving everything; the whales and the ocean following each other independent of whether anything or anyone was around to see it happen throughout the day or in the middle of the night.

Many and Many a Year Ago

You remember they teased you about being born in a factory, that it all—them and you—started early in the day one Friday morning, with dew on the sprigs of grass in the sidewalk cracks and flowers reappearing alongside crumbling brick and mortar, shortly after the first shift had clocked in and begun their mechanical duties unchanged in seven decades and would not change until years after you and they left the factory when management and the local union agreed to test a machine —an industrial-sized press with touchscreens, exhaust hoses, and a generator backed up by a computer in another part of the building where you were not born but where you emerged from.

And you remember they described the factory as assembled out of the cold air, concrete, and steel—colossal blocks of these gray ingredients mashed and squared together— colored with scattered cigarette ashes and encroaching rust and filled with echoes of metal chasing metal like peg-leg pirates dueling on aluminum decks.

In some ways, they are right, and you know your story begins in a place that produced small breakable goods that

brightened or altered the walls of rooms in a house or a garden—
and that it produced you.

In a sense, you were on the conveyor belt snaking across
the southern quadrant of the factory floor. The conveyor belt
stopped, on cue, having appeared from the blue-white haze at the
start of Quality Assurance looking like a science lab of platinum
twists, turns, and drops and the stutters of motors propelling
products. Prior to this point in QA was where Connectivity
Inspectors, twisting switches and plugging cords into a small
outlet mounted on top of the conveyor belt's rails, verified each
unit was operable and behaved as advertised and as the
instruction manual promised. The lamps survived the first crucial
cut here. If they didn't—no juice, bulbs struggling to burn
brightly, sparks and hissing from the cords—they were
immediately placed into a crate labeled PRODUCTION –
CIRCUITRY and would not have been seen again until errors
were fixed, but lamps were never given a third chance to run
through this again. If the lamps were approved, the meter next to
the outlet spiking hard to the right and showing full amps and a
little glowing glass sun enclosed in the A-shaped wireframe, then
a CI clicked the belt back on, and the belt scooted the lamp down
to the next station like messages in bottles bobbing on an
artificial horizon.

And so, the stream of lamps headed towards the last
section of QA stations where a flock of Finishing Inspectors

waited to verify each lamp was free of dents, scratches, chips, and other superficial defects before sending it into the smoke-dark doorway at the opposite end of QA's roller coaster of conveyor belts, where Shipping & Receiving housed its loading docks and delivery trucks. And as she had every Monday through Friday at seven in the morning for the past twenty years, FI 65 watched the line of lamps trickle towards her, each lamp sequentially spaced and timed like the ducks you've seen at carnivals and fairs—those light-weight metal birds folding over as soon as a pellet from a BB gun pings the side; small prizes for the big mallards, big prizes for the small canary-colored ones as the Midway Master tips his hat and cane.

Here, at what was then Coyne-Mecklenburg Manufacturing, the lamps rattled down the line, and FI 65 waited until the conveyor belt's padded square slid under her, at which point she pushed the Pause button on her control box and grabbed the lamp after the belt stopped, examining each of the surfaces suspended in front of her, averaging one unit every minute, taking no more time than that for her evaluation, and after approving the product, slapping a small gold-foil sticker on the bottom and pushing the top green button on her control box, which started the belt again and sent the units towards Shipping & Receiving where a Shipping Specialist carefully rolled the lamps inside bubble wrap, buried them inside a mound of Styrofoam peanuts, and added the shades before taping shut the box and sliding the box onto a pallet a forklift would drive into one of C-M's delivery trucks. A stopwatch on Inspector 65's left ticked on the second the belt stopped for her inspection; a crib sheet on her right, a palm-sized book in a small butterfly-shaped cradle, reminded her what she was responsible for at that point in the process, should she become lost or unsure; but she hadn't opened or felt the urge to refer to any of the stained, dog-eared pages in her time standing there all those years.

But this lamp, your lamp, a lamp that was as common as a cloudless blue sky in spring and was as homogeneous as the lamps that rolled before it and the lamps that waited in line after it, this lamp, your lamp, was in her hands when the conveyor belt jerked to a stop.

And you may recall them telling you someone at the factory had tampered with the bottoms of the new springtime lamps—not all of them, but most. The attacks, as management called them, seemed random. Some of the lamps had marks; others didn't. All of those lamps looked the same, though they were advertised otherwise: unique for that spring season and available at an unbelievable price; Easter-tinted, handcrafted, and European-influenced; "one of a kind." There was no obvious reason why some of the lamps received the tattoo and others didn't.

According to customers who contacted Customer Service, as well as department store managers who filed concerns with C-M, the lamps in question had a total of five letters written with a black felt-tip marker; the first two letters were initials of a first and a middle name, each chased with a period; the remaining three letters made a last name. A few of the customers found the mark "funny," "eerie," "spooky," and "woo-woo," as one woman from Stillwater reported with a ghost story–inspired tone on the phone, or as an elderly gentlemen in Eau Claire chuckled, the name reminded him of high school English classes, of which he wanted no part then and most certainly wanted no part now in the twilight of his life; he wanted to know how the thing on the underside of his lamp could be resolved in a timely manner, either through a refund or receiving a new lamp resembling the vandalized one he had placed on a small table with photos of his dog and his wife and next to his assisted recliner in the living room. You, too, would have known the name right away.

Some of the big department stores, such as Holmgrens, or the local ma-and-pa staples, such as Mansion of Light, which was then a major buyer of C-M products and had labeled itself as Minneapolis' Premier Home Lighting Destination, discounted the lamps, an action, emphasized in their communications with Customer Service, they didn't typically pursue unless the item was part of a heavy, widespread clearance or the store was going under—neither of which, each respective representative said, was happening or was forecasted at that time unless Sales and

Production continued providing damaged items handled by employees who didn't have pride in their work.

You may have heard most of the customers wanted their money back—all or some—which put the squawking birds–loop of businesses in a bind as they pursued each other with regard to who exactly was responsible for what and how much. But because winter had broken down into rain, the Good Lord had died and risen, and the Twins ended April with a 5-21 record, including no wins at home, consumers of the tagged lamps preferred, back then, to want a little more than a source of bright light, perfect for reading or relaxing any day of the week, that rested on a well-known, but highly improbable, American name permanently placed below.

But "Good news," Customer Service reps repeated, referring to the Script for Defaced Lamps management provided, "the marks *are* on the bottom, and no one ever has to see them and probably won't. We can happily send you a replacement, plus shipping and handling." But C-M's top management, not to mention the Board itself, wanted resolution, wanted to move product, and wanted happy customers and purchasers across the tri-state area.

The lamps in question were no larger than a wine bottle —maybe you know this. A hole dominated the middle of the lamp's base and was forged as though a drunk tried forming donuts one late evening, failed miserably, and with no one present to stop him, kept doing so. The lamp was C-M's answer to putting modern, yet accessible, products in the hands of everyday people living in the primary sales regions of Iowa, Minnesota, and Wisconsin. The lamp's colors reflected the time period you know about. One designer in Creative had hoped his Fourth of July–themed lamp would be approved by C-M brass as part of the summer lineup, which was a much bigger draw than Easter/spring but not as popular as Thanksgiving/Christmas, but Product Design and Development's director nixed that, stating it was high time C-M reinvented itself for the up-and-coming generation of buyers, many of whom put away the Frank Lloyd Wright angles and materials and the farmer-outdoorsman-Calvinistic minimalism that propelled C-M in the first part of the twentieth century. Tastes had changed, they told you, and that was, after all, a long time ago.

But you may not know that FI 65's mind had been elsewhere that day at the factory when the marks started appearing as she stood there holding the lamps and compared the weight of them to the weight of her sister's chest rising and falling with each breath inside an intensive care unit at St. Paul Regions Hospital. She stopped the conveyor belt and, moved by her sister's image, took her black felt-tip marker and wrote Elizabeth Anne's initials on the bottom of randomly selected lamps. And she did this knowing she had roughly two minutes until the shift manager opened his office door on the second floor, clanked down the stairs, and searched the labyrinth of conveyor belts, lamps, and workers, aiming his middle-management attention on the sudden broken link in the chain of production—the disciplinary question of Why has your belt stopped? on the tip of his coffee-and-tobacco-smudged tongue.

A buzzer screeched, signaling a conveyor belt in QA had stopped for too long. The office door flung open, and Morning Shift Manager Bates flopped his tie behind him and headed down the stairs. He searched the floor and, when he found the area in question with its buzzer and blinking light, jiggled over like a speed walker needing to urinate. "Everything all right, Alice?"

The other workers glanced up but kept reviewing their own lines of lamps.

"Yes, fine," she answered as she quietly slid the marker into her jeans before slapping the gold sticker F. INPS. 65 – COYNE-MECK. ST. PAUL, MN. on the bottom and next to the initials and last name. "I thought there was a crack around the neck. I wanted to double check." She cranked the conveyor belt back to green, waited for the next lamp in line, and brushing a strand of hair from her eyes, smiled as emotionless as she could.

Bates stared at her and her station, flipped off the warning light and buzzer, sipped from his mug, tipping it back until its words NO TALKIE BEFORE COFFEE disappeared, and left, climbing back upstairs as noise and metal and plastic churned again.

Alice watched the lamp quiver on its padded square until it twisted around the corner and disappeared into the broad doorway of Shipping & Receiving.

After sitting for a few days in the delivery truck at C-M's warehouse, the lamp with the name travelled to the then twenty-second annual Home Furnishings Expo at the Twin Cities Convention Center highlighting upcoming products for the spring season—graduations, Mother's Day, weddings. The other lamps, some of which were marked with the initials and last name, headed to other destinations that have nothing to do with you.

On site and in charge of C-M's booth and show floor at the Expo was a man in his early thirties, sporting a thin mustache, dress shirt, and black slacks, and who was a junior member of, as they were called then, the Bread & Butter sales team handling the most promising and lucrative regions. But his numbers had been down that year, and the old guard let him know he consistently placed last in sales measured by volume, price, and commission percentages. The veterans had selected him, still being the relatively new guy, to man the booth, joking with him that, if he became too scared and pissed his pants while making a big impression on a potential customer, the AstroTurf underneath him would soak it all up—no stain visible.

When the truck finally appeared on that Good Friday morning, the sales rep helped unload, set, and unpack the boxes on the fake-grass floor of the rectangular presentation area. He wandered down the nearby lanes of the competition ("our peers" he was encouraged to call them) and wondered if lamps were his future; his personal favorite was the picnic set, from a company in Mason City, Iowa, with painted clouds and a green field on each piece and when aligned next to each other looked like a complete field. Circling his own booth, he took note of C-M's products, many of which were brightly colored and soft on the eyes, and practiced his pitch that, with summer approaching, it would be a great time to think about installing lights by the pool or outdoor eating areas where people love to spend time with each other. He had his parents and his siblings but no one else— no lover, no filled weekends, nothing other than work on his calendar. The lamp with marks sat on a vanilla-white vitrine behind accessories the sales rep had organized by shape and color; he made sure price tags on any of the items on the floor were obscured. He thought nothing more of what he had accomplished by the time the front doors to the Expo opened to the public.

A few people drifted by; some stopped; some asked questions, which he loved to answer; and some looked at the products for the sake of looking and probably, he knew, and maybe you do, too, comparing prices before humming to themselves, moving their eyes across one show floor and onto the many others before walking again.

It must have been shortly before noon when a woman in her late twenties appeared from the right corner, having left the booth for MW Design with its French countryside–inspired pillows, linens, and beddings. The sales rep did not say anything; he did not approach her right away, taking a cue from the more successful salespeople at C-M that it is best to let customers peruse and, as a salesperson, observe what they're after, the flares they send up.

After a few seconds, he walked over to her and introduced himself with a watered-down upper Midwest accent, which the woman noticed right away, blushed, and commented on it to the sales rep, who, in turn, blushed. The two stared at each other for a few seconds. He asked her what she was looking for in a lamp these days. She told him she wanted to buy something nice for her new apartment, something bright and, as you may know, freeing of the old days she had brought with her. The sales rep suggested some items he had first unloaded. The modestly dressed woman looked at them and then scrunched her face, bypassing all of them. She slid down to the vanilla-white vitrine and lowered her head. She rotated the new lamp in her hands, admired its color and design, and turning it over, laughed out loud.

"Find something you like?"

"Yes," she replied, cradling the lamp.

Standing next to each other, the woman and the sales rep were as plain as you can imagine.

"It's a fine lamp," he began. "One of a kind made right here. It's available only for this season. I love how its glazing breaks apart those gloomy colors of winter. Imagine it in your new apartment, sitting there in the sunshine. And because we're the manufacturer, we offer a discount if you buy directly from us."

"That's good because this thing has a defect." She showed the bottom of the lamp to him.

He took the lamp from her and, squinting, did a double take. The marks were faint, the initials strongly black, the *o* and the *e* in the last name breaking up like smoke. He laughed when he read it.

"Inspector 65 must have been asleep on the job that day." The woman pointed to the gold sticker next to the inked name.

As you may guess, the sales rep was in a pickle: He was stunned his bosses had shipped blemished products for one of the area's biggest events, and there was no way the woman could have marked the lamp because he watched her the whole time she perused the booth. "Maybe it's a prototype, and it snuck into the stack. Sometimes our design department outsources to freelancers who shape possible production types. Or," he joked, tapping the name, "maybe this was his at one point before he became a legend."

"I'm pretty sure lamps weren't like this in the 1800s. If this were his, then it'd be a whole lot more money than this. I like it. It's endearing to me. That name…it's too good. But I'm not paying full price for this."

"I don't have authority to change prices or offer discounts on defects." He grimaced, seeing his name on the leader board for Sales plummet to the bottom from the top three, having jumped there in his head when the woman showed interest in the lamp. "I'm sorry."

"Twenty-five percent off?"

"Definitely not that."

"Fifteen?"

"No."

"Ten."

The man rocked onto his tiptoes. "I'm not supposed to." His knees and shoulders buckled. "Let me see what I can do." He returned with a caterpillar-shaped ashtray matching the lamp in color, not shape or sentiment. "If you would buy this, I could lower the price on the lamp, and it would offset, I think, that, and we can make a deal."

The woman's lips flattened as she snickered. "OK."

The man clapped his hands together and proceeded to ring her up. He wrapped both pieces separately in tissue paper until the lamp resembled a grey bowling pin. He covered the shade with plastic that reminded the woman her father's birthday was on the way—this was back then—and he could use a new lamp because his eyes started to worsen after all those years teaching in her hometown. But the lamp, as you know, ended up hers.

The sales rep offered his business card, which she took, blushing. He could be reached anytime—his office door never closed, especially to her. His hands shook as he handed the receipt to her. He asked her to dinner, not today but soon because he would like a reason to ask his bosses for a Saturday night off; to take her on a date to a restaurant downtown with linen napkins, a sommelier, and a menu devoted solely to dessert.

She said she had started seeing someone and was flattered by the sales rep's offer and his confidence but thought it might be best to say no, stopping any heartache and confusion early, which she politely did, summarizing her situation with her new guy.

The sales rep understood and wanted to ask her out because she was pleasant and kind and had the prettiest eyes he had ever seen; she said thank you and looked away. Last thing he told her: I'll find out, if you want, the story behind the name, the mark on your lamp. That'd be nice, she said, uncapped a pen, and slid his business card back to him with her name and number on it before leaving.

Weeks later the sales rep called the woman and said he had news regarding the marks on the lamp—big news; he knew who did it and this person was indeed an employee at the company where he worked. The woman agreed to meet him at Pawlowski's, which was not the upscale restaurant the sale rep had imagined or hoped for but was a diner sealed in time with red vinyl and chrome, a jukebox with records, and a menu solely dedicated to milkshakes.

Sharply dressed and doused with extra splashes of cologne, he arrived early and stood to greet the woman who, when she arrived wearing a knee-length skirt, flats, and a plaid shirt, smiled as she blushed and started the conversation cordially—mainly about the weather as it was, then, late May, nearing Memorial Day, waves of green floating around them.

After ordering their respective lunches, the sales rep started in with what he knew. Less than two days after the Expo, FI 65 was let go. The woman who bought the lamp was stunned at first but added that it made sense if 65 had been the culprit. The sales rep broke off a large chunk of tuna melt and dragged it through a pool of mustard. The defaced lamps had, he told her, and as you can imagine, cost C-M money and time and trickled onto everyone beneath the Board and upper management. What's more, the sales rep continued, he didn't know FI 65 personally, but he had probably seen her at the company holiday party—the one time all the employees assembled annually yet never mingled with anyone other than those in their divisions. Asking the waitress for change for the jukebox, the sales rep went on to say that QA was in another section far away from Admin and Sales and he rarely had a reason to walk over there and, along with the gold approval sticker next to the inked name and the customers and retail managers contacting Customer Service, FI 65 left a trail back to her. The waitress returned, and the sales rep slid the quarters to the woman who bought the lamp.

"She was fired. Alice Poe."

"What?" the woman replied, keeping one eye on what the sales rep had said and keeping her other eye on the coin slot and the flip-boards of songs.

"Finishing Inspector 65…Alice Poe. They showed up one morning and escorted her to the break room down there in QA, and then they escorted her to the parking lot where they watched her drive away with all her effects. They say she wasn't sad at all, not a goodbye or tears or anything. She left. Twenty years. You got one of the last lamps with marks…they think."

The woman clicked a song. "Alice Poe," she echoed. "Well, that explains a lot. I wonder why she did it."

"I don't know." The sales rep fidgeted on his side of the booth. "So yeah, I wanted to meet up and fill you in. How's the lamp?"

"You didn't call me only because of the lamp." She looped her hair behind her ear and weaved her shoulders as Roy Orbison sang. "We could have talked about this on the phone. It didn't require us meeting anywhere for lunch."

The sales rep leaned back and smiled.

"The lamp is sitting on my little end-table by my couch. It looks great, and it works, unless there's another surprise waiting."

"Good." He quickly stuffed a handful of french fries into his mouth.

"It's a funny, quirky thing to see, and I love it. I love that mark. But mainly, it reminds me of my father who's a teacher and said we get things in pieces, some of them loose but nearby, others left to find. I love that it's a misfit, but I'm the only one enjoying it right now."

As the sales rep nodded, she asked him about his job, what led him to C-M and selling lamps, what he likes, doesn't like, where he hoped to be in six months, one year, five years.

"I want to be a good person," he replied. "And make enough money to live humbly and without debt and to travel, but it doesn't have to be international because there's so much in this county that I haven't seen." He mentioned Yellowstone, back then, which the woman did too, her eyes brighter, and they drew a map with a pen he carried in his folder and, after starring where they were then, condensed the country inside a napkin, implying the four main points: Maine's oven mitt in the top right, Florida dangling in the bottom right, the broad hide of Texas covering the mid-section, the infinite stretch of the West coast— California, Oregon, Washington blurred into one continuous border defined only by the ocean it fell into. Across the middle of the country, in the open space of the middle, the sales rep drew a car and music notes bubbling from the inside because, as you know, it was, and is, the most American thing to do.

After he was hired, he told her, he saw the archives at C-M and some of the first lamps they used to make. According to company history, C-M started and took off because of a shortage of lamps, thanks to an iron-ore strike in which most of Chicago and northern Indiana shut down factories and laid off workers. Back in those days, he told her, all the lamps were handcrafted, because this was before the mass webbing of machinery, and not to romanticize it, he qualified, but things were made slower and with precision and care and artistry. One old lamp in particular caught his eye on the tour—a lamp with a glass reservoir for oil at the back that looked like, given its size and all-black matte finish, it belonged on a military tank. But, he said, it had one of C-M's signature features at the time. He said you had to look at the handle, where a flat piece of scrimshaw, about as long and narrow as a breadstick, lay embedded: a dove with an olive branch between its beak flying over a rainbow, all of this in blue-black ink.

Leaning closer to her, Who? he asked aloud, half rhetorically, half directed at her in hope for an answer she may have. Who, your father repeated, after finishing his milkshake and wiping his hands, figured out oil from the blubber could be used for lamps, the baleen could be fashioned into teeth for combs and brushes, and the bones, once stripped clean, he asked your mother, were suitable for telling a story?

Martingale

First thing she starts in about after the two of them break away from the others—her calling out his name, telling him good morning and how happy she is to see him again and rubbing his neck's soft slopes and leaning over his right ear, whispering, her voice's volume rising when she's close, falling when she pulls away and acknowledges the others circling in front of them, hanging out by the fence, and staring at the two of them—is how much she has to tell him before she leaves, and Peter hears how it's another Wednesday, gray getting grayer and the cold getting colder, the nights at their longest now, Christmas less than three days away, and Caroline will miss him but also can't wait to get out of here for the holiday break and be with her mom and dad, for a few hours with each of them, but she's not sure if she'll reach out to Conner, or if she should at all.

And because it's Wednesday, she's nervous, indecisive about calling Conner again, getting his voicemail again, him not returning any of her calls, and she has wondered if he returns her calls but maybe the receptionist and the staff aren't passing them on to her by accident or, given her recent mood change, by choice. She tells Peter she still doesn't like feeling this way and many times throughout the day she believes this is happening—they are restricting Conner's access to her; restricting her access to Conner; she's not *that* crazy. This habit of calling Conner every Wednesday as one of the two weekly ten-minute calls she's allowed to make and clicking into his voicemail and not hearing back from him keep her, she knows, from continuing to reshape her story. He remains prominent and fastened to the plot of her new life.

Peter leans in as Caroline fluctuates between the future, where she bounces off a ceiling of uncertainty, and the old days, where, after hitting resistance, she dives back down onto an unstable but familiar support of how she used to be. But the past can be jumped into or jumped over, as she has seen since being with Peter. Habits, behaviors, and patterns she's repeated. And he has heard a lot about them, her desire to uncover and explore more of them, she has said to him, reforming them through her writings, talks, and responsibilities during her stay at the ranch, especially walking outside and doing the exercises with the pretty golden boy himself, Peter.

And then her voice cuts off, accentuated by her head quickly turning over her shoulder, her flat and thin, black hair twisting around, its cherry-red tips following, because they are no longer alone.

"Hey, finish and clean up before leaving, OK?" Glenn says, a brightness glowing in his baritone. "Please and thank you." He nods to Peter and Caroline who scrapes mud onto the ground.

"OK," she answers, dropping Peter's hoof. Her breathing shifts from short, controlled pulses of chit-chatting to long, sustained breaths pulling her elsewhere.

After Glenn leaves, Caroline peeks around the corner of the stable and looks at Peter—no one paying any attention to them—and she faces the back of the stable with its wood and metal shelves holding tack supplies. The lock on the toolbox glints. The smells of straw and dust, cold leather, and metal circling animals fill the air.

Wiped clean with a towel, the farrier knife shines like a silver question mark in her hand. Caroline hasn't returned it, and Peter remains silent watching her. She inhales deeply before she walks to the toolbox, opens it, places the knife inside, clangs the lid shut, locks it, and snaps the elastic keychain around her arm, pinching her hoodie's black sleeve.

She jogs back to Peter, glances at him, and picks up where she left off, plugging back into her loop again, her breathing accelerating again, words to her stories coming back on: how she's still struggling with Conner in her life—maybe because two months hasn't been enough; maybe three months won't be enough; maybe because it's the holidays, struggling with him more than usual, like a ghost that will neither go away nor respond no matter how many times she's reached out to it and asked to talk.

Returning to the stable, Glenn sets a box down on the table and surveys the work area, pausing on the tack supplies and toolbox.

"I'm ready," Caroline tells him like an interruption. She unwraps the keychain from her arm and hands it to him.

Before sliding it into his pocket, Glenn stares at it before looking at Caroline. "It was pretty quiet in here, especially for the two of you." He hangs a brush on a hook by the toolbox and double-checks it's locked. He smiles without showing his teeth.

Caroline returns a similar smile, her eyes blinking rapidly.

"A'right," Glenn says, "let's hit those trails."

Lagging behind, she sighs louder to Peter, saying she knew it, she knew this would happen, she saw it coming. Chaperones. So unfair. "I shouldn't let it ruin our time together," she mumbles in his ear, as she loosens the halter and holds the bit in place until Peter bites down.

• • •

Seven weeks into the three-month program at New Life Ranch, Caroline is the loquacious one—few among her peers. But she saves the bulk of talking for when it's Peter and her in the woods, which the last few outings have changed with Glenn tagging along. She has covered all of her personal topics with Peter—from her crushes ("*Twilight*, which I know is so old") to what she thinks of the others, especially the two girls, in her group. On and on she has practiced with Peter her breaking down and rebuilding that time in October, sneaking out of her bedroom to be with the one boy who had noticed her.

Peter has heard all of it from her, the good, the bad, the old, and the new in the time he and Caroline have spent together on the trails or working on their exercises in the arena. "Metaphors and mirrors," Peter has heard Dr. Bonnie and Glenn call them.

Caroline has told Peter the original version of what brought her to where he is; where they both are: She couldn't sneak back into her bedroom through the window that night, and taking the emergency key from under the garden gnome, she opened the back door. "God, the screaming," she has recalled many times, Peter chugging along next to her as she covered her face early on. "It was so loud…so, so loud. I nearly passed out from just *that*." She reminds the Palomino she looks forward to as much time as she can get with him.

As Glenn, Caroline, and Peter walk toward the trails snaking behind the arena, Peter whinnies, tightens his ribs and stride the closer he gets to the other teens in Caroline's group working with another horse. Brushing Peter's neck, Caroline whispers in his ear, "We won't be here long."

Dr. Bonnie has lined up a group exercise for the three teens lounging about. Buttercup is supposed to be on her way over from the stable, thanks to the efforts of the other teens, but as part of the exercise, they are not allowed to touch the sleek bay mare or to simulate they have a treat if Buttercup does or does not follow through with what they ask of her.

"Glad that's not us today," Caroline says, patting Peter whose whinny is louder when Mark and Alysha walk by. She pats him again.

"Stupid horse won't come over here," Mark moans to Buttercup and the others in the group. "Athhole."

"*Mark*," Glenn reprimands, cocking his head as his large body creaks the arena's fence, thick forearms on the white wood beams. "Come on, buddy. Be better than that. Use what we've worked on."

Alysha and Kaycee smirk and laugh out loud whenever Mark talks.

Clouds and the morning gray burning off, the sun shining for what will be the shortest day of the year, Glenn pulls a tube of sunscreen from his jacket pocket. After smearing his face and neck, he offers the tube to Caroline, who shakes it off as Peter feels her tug the reins, leading him away from the greasy counselor. Glenn slurps from his coffee mug and bites into the last chunk of apple before resealing the sandwich bag and dropping it with the sunscreen tube in the side pocket of his cargo pants.

"You should've tothed that to me," Mark teases, standing halfway between the bay mare and the fence. "Buttercup, come here, Buttercup."

Buttercup stands solid in the middle of the arena and stretches her head into the clumps of remaining green grass, ignoring Mark as he flags her down with his red ball cap; ignoring Ashlyn and Kaycee hovering on either side of her, arms up, laughing and trying to move her.

"You wish, buddy. You can do it. I've seen you do it before." Glenn makes a face at Dr. Bonnie who returns a similar fatigue. "OK, we're off. We'll be back by lunch."

Caroline pulls herself into the saddle when Dr. Bonnie smiles and waves goodbye to them. Her heels tap Peter's sides; she clicks her tongue. Buttercup whinnies in the middle of the arena, having wandered farther away from Mark, Kaycee, and Alysha. Peter whinnies back, tail pluming. Off he and Caroline go toward the trails, speeding up as they glide away from the arena, the stable, and the open fields by the main facility. They head into the woods, leaving Glenn behind and forcing him to run to catch up.

• • •

Peter was the first horse Caroline knew by name and wanted to know; the others in her group fell away. He made his way to her when they were at the arena or stable. Glenn said nothing is earned until they've learned the horse's name and until the horse responds when called by that name. "At the very least, walk away from here with that."

During introductions in November, Alysha reached out to Peter. "Horse," her voice rasped. "Oh, this is perfect for me." Her eyes rolled above the shadows under them like little purple-black wings over her pierced nose. She turned to her fellow teens, Dr. Bonnie, and Glenn. "I'm the heroin addict, unless anyone else wants to claim it, too." She raised a small, doll-like hand sliding out from the sleeve of a red-and-black flannel shirt. "My drug of choice," the nineteen-year-old continued, turning to Peter and thrusting her neck at him, to which he retreated his head and ears and whinnied away from her.

"Straight up four-twenty for me," said Kaycee before Peter shimmied his head toward her, smelling her. "OK, and some pharm parties. My uncle's Vike and OC." She cleared her throat. "And this is my second…third?…time back. Hey, Dr. Bonnie. Hey, Glenn."

"I huffed," Mark said. "Spray paint, thinner, nail polish, you know. I can't say certain words because of it. Rotted my brain and tongue and mouth." Mark traced a skeletal finger over his jawline and up to his earlobe before immediately returning it to his jacket pocket.

Alysha asked, "Like what?"

"Double eth."

"Did you say meth?" snickered Kaycee. "Double meth?"

"Seriously, are you from the four-one-seven?"

"Nah, Warrenton." The sixteen-year-old looked at the ground and adjusted his Cardinals ball cap. "Double eth."

Walking over to Caroline, Peter jutted his head between her and the others. She rubbed his nostrils as she stepped forward to talk, placing her chin on the hard bridge of his nose. She shrugged and blushed. "Um, you know. Some Triple C, boys, bad decisions. Which went a little too far one night."

"Boys and bad decisions always go together and always go too far." Alysha wrinkled her nose when Peter cozied up next to Caroline, his haunches glancing her chin.

Dr. Bonnie placed her hands in prayer position in front of her legs. "Let's move on to a team-building exercise."

She led them to one of the arena's hurdles dropped on its lowest pegs, inches off the ground. Twisting behind it, long plastic tubes formed an alley, inside of which Glenn had placed red buckets filled with alfalfa cubes, slices of apples and carrots, and peppermints, Peter's favorite.

"Make two stacks," Dr. Bonnie said, motioning with her head. "One with words describing your past…the decisions and behaviors that brought you here. And one with words you want to work on."

Glenn smiled and handed out index cards and Sharpies.

Mark, Alysha, and Kaycee finished after brief minutes of silence and scribbling. Pieces of paper crumpled by her feet, Caroline was the last to say she was done. One by one, they took the roll of tape from Glenn and attached the past to the buckets and the future to the hurdle.

For ninety minutes Peter wandered out of the alley, stopped after walking a few yards, backed up, whinnied to Buttercup, farted, stomped one hoof, extended one leg at an angle, and threw his head up and down. Once they got him moving forward, toward the hurdle, he reached the first bucket and knocked it over with a hoof, spilling and filching some of the apple slices inside. He wandered to the next one and knocked it over with his snout. Peppermints.

Glenn helped the four teens spin Peter around. "Get him to the hurdle."

"Dude won't go," Mark said, short of breath.

"Well, work with him. Don't control him. *Ask* him."

Peter snorted.

"Tell him what you want."

Alysha sighed and crossed her arms.

Peter butted into Caroline. Her eyes aligned with his— dark auburn pearls on dark auburn pearls. She twisted her mouth side to side; she looked away. Peter whinnied, curled his lips at her, and raised his head toward leaves turning into flames and waiting to fall.

She said, "I want you to follow me and don't stop for anything in the buckets, K? We're going right to there."

Peter lowered his head and blew out his nose, launching globs of snot onto her shirt. He started urinating in front of her.

"Nice," Kaycee murmured.

"Watch out!" Mark covered his mouth with his arm. "I think he's gonna pith on you!"

"Got a fave already," Alysha said, laughing with the others. "Teacher's pet."

"Peter," Caroline soothed, coaxing him and putting a hand on his reins.

They moved down the lane, past the buckets. Before the session ended, he followed her to the end of the alley—the hurdle between them.

"Next time we're out here get him over that," Glenn said, stepping in and taking off the bridle. "We'll do it lots of times. Without the tack, and then with."

Caroline and Peter stared at each other after he shook his head free.

• • •

Reaching the curve of the trail running against the facility's property, Caroline sighs in the cool air. Peter rebalances his stride whenever she adjusts herself in the saddle. She talks to him and to herself; his blonde tail swishes. "If I see him, it'll be different this time." The old story winds and rewinds inside her, tightened around uncertainty—how it'll be odd for her to be let out in a few days for Christmas only to return and finish up the next few weeks and then to be let out again at the end of January. For good she tells him.

"Once I'm done here I'm not coming back. I want you to know that." She sits up and down. "GED. Get a job. I'm getting an apartment with my step-sister in St. Louis." Silence before she clears her throat. "Kaycee says I'll be *back*-back, like there's nowhere else to go once you've been here. 'Spin dry,' she said."

Peter's stride steadies along the dirt and rocks.

"I mean, maybe they'll let me visit you."

He backs up, twitches a little, and spins his ears behind his mane when Glenn's voice calls to them.

"Oh God, here he comes."

Caroline lets Peter drift off the main trail. He lowers his head, sniffs the ground, and gnaws a fallen pit before spitting it out.

"You guys are off to the races today," Glenn pants. The remaining hair on his head waterfalls down the base of his collar.

"We can't be alone?"

Peter rotates his ear when Glenn counters. "Come on, don't be that way. I love walking with you two."

Caroline's breathing pulses; she grips the reins tighter until Peter whinnies and shakes his head.

The three of them trudge along the trail, leaves crunching under them, and the ones the wind hasn't pulled off trees flicker like burnt flags.

Breaking a long silence, Caroline says, "I know why it's us out here."

"Why?"

"So you can give me some one-on-one talk about being hung up with Conner. You brought me out here to 'talk' about it by not talking about it."

"No. No talk. We're just walking. Like normal."

Peter whinnies.

They walk a few more yards in silence. Caroline wants to speed up, but Peter paces himself.

"I know you've changed. We all know you've changed since being here." He turns his pale face up at her. "You've changed...*forward*. We want you to stick with that. It's real easy to slide back. Believe me, I know. We know that change has come from you."

Caroline inhales and exhales deeply.

They drift in minutes of silence.

"Why did you look at me?" she asks.

"When?"

"Back at the stable, when I was done getting him ready."

"When I walked back?"

"Yeah."

"You two are always chatting it up. It was quiet for the two of you."

Peter snorts.

"You gave me a look. You totally, like, stared at me. It was judgmental."

"I'm sorry if it came across that way."

"Was it the knife?"

Glenn grabs Peter's bridle and stops them on the trail. The counselor clears his throat and stands at an angle in front of Peter's head and pats his cheek. "Yes, it was."

"Really? You think that? Peter's been my responsibility for how long now?"

"And he is. But Conner *is* still around."

"You don't trust me now?"

"That's not it."

"It must be if you're, like, watching me do my job. A job *you* and Dr. Bonnie gave me."

Some birds stretch their smoke-gray V in the blue sky. Peter whips his head about.

"It's not *only* about trust. Trust is a small part. What it's about is keeping *you* moving forward, and *you* wanting to keep moving forward."

"You, of all people here, don't think I know that by now?"

"I know you know."

"Well?" Caroline's voice spikes, to which Peter whinnies.

"You're right. I should have given you some more space. No one is stopping Conner from contacting you. And no one is stopping you from contacting him." Glenn clicks his tongue, starts moving, but Peter stamps his legs, flicks his tail, remains in the same spot.

Caroline brushes his neck and clicks her tongue. The three move again.

"Not gonna lie," she says minutes later. "I could have taken it. Part of me wanted to. It was in my head. Like those cartoons with the angel on one shoulder and the devil on the other."

"I know what that's like. I've been there. And I'm glad you made a good decision."

Caroline snickers. "It's not that sharp anyway. It gets out Petey Boy's mud."

Glenn chuckles back. "I know."

The air's crispness intensifies in pockets along the trail. Degrees of browns, oranges, and grays quiver under a bright blue sky.

Caroline's shoulders collapse, rounding under a heavy, invisible weight, causing Peter to stand still. "Why won't he talk to me?" She cries underneath the black cloud forming over the horizon of her voice.

Peter turns his head toward her.

"Is it OK if I do this?" Glenn's voice buoys.

Caroline nods as Glenn holds her hand on the saddle horn. She forces a chuckle through her tears, sniffling and blowing her nose into her hoodie's sleeve.

"Go in a little at a time," he says. "You can't get it all back at once. It's a real blessing to be able to do that."

Peter strengthens when Caroline slumps and when his reins loosen in her hands.

• • •

A week and a half before the Thanksgiving break, Caroline made her first revision. She and Peter trotted on a swath of trails between the woods and the arena. The majority of the tree leaves had changed color and started falling.

"You can shape it like a story," she told Peter about Dr. Bonnie's description of a person's life. She leaned in and started telling him about that night when she screamed after sneaking back in through the mudroom in her mom's house. "I was tripping so hard," she grimaced as Peter bobbed his head under her voice warbling with each crooked step they took. "I made so much noise, but I thought I was being quiet and wouldn't get caught. Stupid."

The physical location of Conner's locker, she described to Peter, was like any of the other lockers along the purple-and-yellow halls at the home of the Panthers and Lady Panthers. He had transferred in from another school. He wasn't a jock. He wasn't on the honor roll.

"'It'd be fun to hang out with you. You're cute. Trouble-fun,'" she repeated Conner's words the day he started talking to her and looking at her, pulling her out from floating in the middle layer of students who were in neither the top nor the bottom. When September ended, he had told her how much he loved her, repeating it, their relationship resembling a ride at the local amusement park: fast, slow, faster, slower, forward, backward, round and round, yelling in the air, chasing each other in an undulating, never-ending circle.

And then it was Halloween, and over cocktails of alcohol, acid, weed, and Dexedrine at a party in the basement of strangers, Caroline caught Conner kissing a girl from his old school. "I never really loved you," Conner, dressed as a zombie, mumbled to Caroline, pushing her away, smearing the bumblebee paint on her face. "I want to tell him something in my new version. But I don't know what," she said to Peter before repeating that in front of him with Dr. Bonnie and Glenn and her group one November day in the arena.

And when she changed it, she didn't walk home by herself through a neighborhood she barely knew: She calls a cab, and once back at her mom's house, knowing full well she still has disrespected her mom and her rules, she still sneaks back in through the mudroom, still knocks over a chair, still cries as she pleads with herself and the ghosts in front of her, is still confronted by her mom, but the yelling between them subsides, and Caroline, wiping her eyes, throat dry, chemicals trickling through her bloodstream and assembling and reassembling her hopes, fears, and guilt, walking through her own private maze of the living and the dead, doesn't rush out of her bedroom and head for the garage. She doesn't find the box opener. She doesn't walk back inside, drifting past her mom again, who's on the phone and blaming her father for causing all this, for leaving them. She doesn't turn the bathtub's hot water on full—steam sticking to the small bathroom's mirror and chrome. She doesn't lock the door behind her. Her mother doesn't force open the door. Neither of them screams. The paramedic does not bandage her wrists.

• • •

Deeper into the woods they go near the last straight shot of trail before it curls up and then down, ending where it started.

"Bathroom," Caroline says to Glenn. She stops them all, slings her leg off the saddle, and adjusts her black hoodie before making her way to the edge of the woods.

Glenn's expression neither gives permission nor stops her. "Caroline," he moans, watching her shuffle into the leaves and further away from his flat-lined response echoing in the air.

"I gotta go, Glenn!"

Peter snorts and shakes his head, looks over to where Caroline walked into the woods. Rustling, rustling, rustling. Quiet. More quiet. Faint rustling. Peter's ears rotate. Arms crossed between his small chest and robust belly, sighing, Glenn paces back and forth alongside Peter and the small curtain of tans and oranges behind which Caroline has disappeared. Peter backs away with a whinny from Glenn, whose hands drop to his side. Another whinny from Peter, and Glenn starts in for the spot in the woods but then stops.

"Took you long enough."

"I knew you were watching," she smirks as she trudges back. "Can't do it with an audience."

Peter's head turns toward them.

Glenn sighs as he looks at Caroline.

"What?" she asks.

"You know I have to check."

"So it's like jail now?" Scowling, Caroline yanks the reins from Glenn once she returns to the saddle where her body twitches.

The arguing heats up between the two of them, more talking from Glenn, more snap-defense from Caroline, and Peter feels her hands whip down. She wants to head back faster. Glenn reminds Caroline of the past few months.

"*Not* friends," she snaps. "Counselor and weirdo."

Glenn tries calming her, reminding her that's not true; that's not how anyone here has ever seen her; that that kind of response is old and not her today—she's come so far since being here, wanting her to remember decisions are day to day; and with the struggle she's been having with Conner, she can, and should, get back to opening up again in Group.

The arena and stable ahead, they stagger back, Caroline in the saddle trying to speed them up, swaying as Peter sways, Glenn walking next to them, tugging the reins to slow them down—an earthly version of the Holy Family coming in from afar and stopping at a common stable. Peter jerks his head and rips off a few farts as they pass Kaycee, whose rambling fades in and out like a radio station. Alysha is on the hunt for discarded cigarette butts to smoke. Mark's voice intensifies as he rides Buttercup for the first time on the dirt track along the edge of the arena. "This is so badath!" He's jostled about, his ball cap on backward.

Peter heads straight for the bag of alfalfa cubes and peppermints waiting for him near the empty stalls under the metal roof littered with acorns, twigs, and leaves, near the bare trees backlit by the sun where "Thank you"—Caroline's whisper —is the last to arrive.

Transplant

GRAND RE-OPENING SOON! exclaimed the sign above the heavily plastic-wrapped and taped double doors leading into the main foyer of Velvet Glove. I walked into its fragmented ghosts of Wildcats, the club's previous incarnation, but the contractors working inside had already assembled the Jazz Age elements and started replacing the derrick- and pump-jack-shaped themes, mirrors, chrome, and sparkling décor on the remaining walls and booths for brass and gold sconces and polished dark wood and inlays management bragged about to me months ago. I brushed past a lineup of blinking modems on the bar and new cash registers set up for wireless transactions. A man wearing a yellow hardhat lowered a pallet of frosted and etched glass panes a few feet from me. Fleur-de-lis.

Management motioned to me after I nearly tripped over extension cords and sidestepped a concrete mixer and a stack of lumber. They sat at a small round table set between the main stage, with its old wood flooring ripped out and metal support beams exposed, and bungee-wrapped chairs detailed with intricate wood slats. After standing up, all three of them lowered their coffee cups, jiggled their laptops, and passed out the day's itinerary and goals and a notepad and a pen for me. No more emails and video talks—our first official meeting as bosses and new employee on my first day on the job.

Artificial Eye Mike introduced himself first. He said he was fifty-percent owner of Velvet Glove, and he offered this fact in the middle of a long welcome to me, asking if I had found a place to live (yes, on this side of the river, near the Warehouse District), how I liked the city (still getting used to being back in this part of the country, but my parents were happy we were closer), if I had any BBQ yet (not yet, but I planned on it). He pointed upstairs to his second-floor office overlooking the main floor where we sat. He said he's not an office-windows guy or a micro-manager, doesn't plan on being either, especially because he's set in his ways at his age, and his plain white tablecloth of a dress shirt reflected all that.

He introduced the second owner, also named Mike, whose class ring squeezed his ring finger and who owned twenty-five percent of VG.

"And Chef," Artificial Eye Mike said to me, "this is Claire Sarsgaard, who is our third owner and our GM. And she owns the final twenty-five percent."

"I'm so pleased to meet you in person," the tall brunette GM said, shaking my hand. "I'm excited for all you have planned for us, and I look forward to our many challenges and, of course, successes from our hard work at the rebranding and…"

A saw cutting behind us broke her speech.

She winced as though beneath a dentist's drill and adjusted her black jacket. "Our upgrades are upgrading as I speak…apparently. Anyway, we've already crossed off our logo from our to-do list, which I'm sure you noticed on the way in."

"I did."

"Good. We're close to finishing the stage area and the lighting and the locker room for the entertainers…not just girls anymore." Closing her eyes, she held up her slender finger with a large diamond on it. "Trained *en-ter-tain-ers*." Her finger punctuated the accents. "And we have those items we're tackling, and now we need to cross off that kitchen of ours and its food… *your* kitchen, Chef."

"We're going to capitalize on the changes around us," Artificial Eye Mike joined in. "All those retrofits of century-old warehouses and buildings between Walker and Seventh and the river. Lots of potential, minutes from shops, restaurants, galleries, and historic attractions. Even in this economy we're going to do it. Polished and refined."

Rotund Mike pushed up his glasses and nodded in agreement with Artificial Eye Mike. He added phrases pitched by the area's developers, real-estate agents, and city hall's marketing department I had read about before agreeing to this job.

"More implicit, less explicit," Claire said. "Music. Artsy. Playful."

Something heavy crashed behind her, followed by cursing and chuckling.

"We need a TV crew in here to document what we're doing. *Flip This Old Strip Club*," she said before quickly correcting and closing her eyes. "Not a strip club."

All three, as I listened and sipped my coffee, remained adamant about pushing forward with rebranding Velvet Glove and filling it with happy, sophisticated patrons in a safe environment electrified by a live band playing big-band sounds, comedy routines between each number, and the dancers. To their credit, management's story face-to-face did not veer from what we had talked about when hundreds of miles had been between us.

"And you," the dark feather-headed GM said to me, "are going to help us distinguish ourselves from everyone else." She stared at me with a crooked smile.

We stood up from the table and took a quick tour of the facility deeply embedded in demolition and renovation, Artificial Eye Mike and Claire leading the way. Ducking under a jungle of wires, I inspected the kitchen with them. It reeked of grease, fires, and bits of food that should have been discarded long ago. There were rat droppings by the refrigerator, which I refused to open because cream-like goo oozed between the deteriorating sealant and the rusted, dented door.

"Open-space kitchen and prep area," Artificial Eye Mike said, pretending to knock out damaged walls and crusty appliances with his hand.

"Let the patrons see what's happening in the kitchen," Claire added. "It'll be like any of the big restaurants in New York, San Francisco, or L.A. Modern touches, amenities, and high-quality ingredients."

Rotund Mike's cheeks wobbled as he nodded and threw in, with his Southern accent, "Or like Emeril's in New Orleans."

I picked up an old inventory list and menu and hoped the menu could simply be called Menu and no longer Grub and Bub.

"Not just upgrade the menu," VG's management emphasized in unison. An overhaul, a complete start-over from scratch. I scribbled notes on my pad, and what they said still lined up with what we had talked about during my interview process. Farm to table. Local ingredients. Seasonal items. Relationships with area farms, farmers, and ranchers. Hit the farmers' market. "And we need it all *yesterday*," they chimed.

"We're not cruising frozen-food aisles anymore or finding something for the microwave like the old crew used to do," Artificial Eye Mike said. "We're talking prepping menus, prepping food, slow cooked, three- to five-course meals that match the atmosphere of the club, the season, and the drinks. Cohesion with what's out there." He threw his head to the refurbished stage and the conductor's box installed with the whirring sounds of bolts and a drill.

"Speaking of your crew," Claire interjected. "It's your show. You're welcome to clean house on the old staff. Hire anyone you feel matches what you and we are doing here." The tall, power-suited GM glanced at Mike and Mike before smiling at me. "A brand-new image. No more of the old days. You're our… *the*…executive chef."

By the end of that Monday afternoon, the four of us agreed to a frenzied month for me to finalize ingredients, sources, budgets, and at my insistence, a chance for the old Wildcats' kitchen staff to try out. I told the three owners I have little time and need anyone at this point who has basic food skills to help, but I also told them I would set up simple but necessary tests to separate the wheat from the chaff and would have a contingency plan if all else failed. Chopping, cutting, plating, saucing, grilling, pairing, preparing—who can handle my demands and who can contribute. "We will be ready in time for the big Valentine's Day celebration," I promised, my eyes catching the glare on the freshly shoveled snow in the parking lot behind the kitchen.

"That's what we want to hear, boss lady," they replied.

• • •

Tulsa was not my first choice for where to start my life and career again in my late-thirties, in all things reemerging from a recession, even if the details of the job appealed to me and reflected my skills and experience. I knew about the city because it was regional to where I had grown up (a straight-shot from my adolescent home), and I also knew of it because of Will Rogers and blues and country (part of Dad's private museum of cultural holdings and memories); Garth Brooks, Gary Busey, Hanson, *The Outsiders* ("Stay gold, Pony Boy."); and Route 66 (Mom loved the antique stores along the Mother Road)—and because my home state's beloved Razorbacks battled the Golden Hurricanes in college sports.

Before the job at Velvet Glove appeared to me, I teetered on the precipice of quicksand debt and another year of credit-card living, dead-end job searches, and the narrowing hallway of decisions and my livelihood dependent on a selection of doors rapidly evaporating the longer I waited. Food, I had reasoned before all this, was something everyone needed, even the frothy indulgences and sweet extravagances I helped make, and approaching my thirty-fourth birthday, I was confident enough my job and the food Lumina 212 provided in Manhattan's Flatiron District were insulated and the clientele who helped keep the dollar signs plentiful on the menus would be the same clientele who would help keep the doors open.

But then it happened. My hours shrank until the restaurant shut its doors and permanently turned off its gas ranges, freezers, and refrigerators. Gone were the days of smoking cigarettes behind the restaurant and drinking cold bottles of Stella after the last dish was cleaned. No more saucing, garnishing, and plating food for the runners. No more chatting with my line cooks. No more *chef de partie* and my name Eva Michelle following that hard-earned title. It was all over. The investors had suffered from financial stalactites dripping from economic charts every time the markets rose and set with the sun, and they dismissed the veteran executive chef, my colleagues, and me. My friends, who had lost jobs in other industries, joked this was the opportunity for us to real-world test, for some of them, their feminist convictions or, for others, to re-visit their old-fashioned prudence that college and the Big Apple had disintegrated, and strip for money, but I had and still have no body for that, and I was not going to pay for anything plastic and stereotypical, to which one of my friends said "seriously, none of that mattered anyway" because the recession was also stripping the stripping industry. Bankers, Wall Street employees, and tech moguls weren't filling the clubs like they did when the economy looked more like gilded pools and not backwater floods mixing sewage leaks. One of the world's oldest professions was not immune to monetary calamity.

After promising myself one year to get out of where I was; after moments and months of considering working as a butcher in the meat/seafood department in a grocery store, clocking in and out at a fast-food chain, or entering grad school for any subject that would not fully hold my interest but would accumulate more debt; after consecutive weeks of an inbox empty of serious or half-serious prospects; after Capitalism sent the trains of Rent and Bills toward me at break-neck speed while I was tied to the tracks; after feeling sick for all the times my cynicism helped me throw snide comments against the phrases Do What You Love – Love What You Do and Create Your Own Success, the one and only option in my dearly loved field appeared. The irony of what my friends had joked about plopped down next to me when Velvet Glove and I found each other.

The tagline that drew me in? EXEC CHEF NEEDED FOR REBRANDED ENTERTAINMENT CLUB. As I read the description, I soon realized VG's management sought transforming the club into something "your grandparents would attend" (their pitch), in addition to providing not a new restaurant in town but, according to About Us on the job description, "a new, classy touch on an old concept."

After a little digging around, I discovered Velvet Glove was previously known for thirty-plus years as Wildcats and, playing off the area's oil and petroleum industry, had offered three kinds of lap dances—Regular, Mid-Grade, and Premium, all available in the Oil Baron room. The former club was also a seedy home to prostitution, drug sales, and regular busts by vice squads. But I was sold on management's statement of wanting not only tasteful, sensual burlesque dancing that was "fun, entertaining, and empowering" and included women of all shapes and sizes, wherein teasing, titillation, and laughter were the goals, not exploitation, but also providing "high-quality food created and managed by our executive chef who, commensurate with experience, will have control on menus, ingredients, and kitchen staff." But I did pause when I came across the club's location—a part of the country I swore I'd never live in again. But the cordial and professional emails between VG's management and me kept reeling me back. "You're one of our top candidates," they confided after the last videoconference interview.

I stared at the job description, the possibility, and the excitement emitting from our interactions; my brain's cocktail of happy-making chemicals tingled under my skin. I stared at the location; the cocktail dripped and dragged. I reminded myself I had no other options. I stared at the job description one more time. Throwing my hands in the air and saying to myself, Why not? I may be there ten years. I may be there ten days.

As celebration for earning the job, I got a tattoo of Mars on the inside of my left arm and, under it, the symbol for Aries (my birth-sign)—warrior, tenacious, battle-ready. My friends cheered and reminded me of their joke months ago. I told my parents my new full-time, full-benefits, forty-hours-plus job needed my skills and proficiencies under one roof—I'd be an executive chef, my own boss in my own kitchen. It helped that I clarified Velvet Glove will "not be your typical place" and (I quoted the website) it will be "'classy and sassy, not nasty.'" They were happy I had found a job that aligned with me, and they laughed at the club's name, its theme, and its presentation to the world at large, as I had to laugh. Security, I told them, will be sharply dressed, and dress shirts and sport coats must cover their tattoos, and Velvet Glove will be a smoke-free establishment. A no-nonsense policy firmly in place. "Well, that's great. Glad to hear it's all worked out for you, *Chef*," Dad emphasized. "We knew you'd pull it off. We're so proud of you."

• • •

Three of the five original kitchen help from the Wildcats days showed up for training and testing, but I asked one of them to leave because he stunk of alcohol. The two brothers remaining impressed me—in particular, the older one, who listened to my instructions and was willing to adapt to what I wanted from him and with the plates I had envisioned. *Lots of potential, hard worker, quick learner* I noted. *Very capable.* No criminal records for either brother. Just a few write-ups and run-ins with the old Wildcats management for the older one, which I could relate to. Fiery and tenacious. Like me.

After dry runs, teaching moments, and long days and nights with my newly fashioned and hard-tested crew, I was pleased with what they could do in such little time and under my constant barking and tweaking. The two brothers met my standards. They pulled off some amazing things. And management was pleased with what I presented to them. The dishes they loved, and the techniques and presentations they praised—and all achieved under a tight deadline. They approved my budgets and my gear, but their green-light attitude quickly changed when I told them I was keeping the two brothers for my staff.

"They can do what's asked of them," I said, motioning to the meals management had praised. "I'll scramble to find someone with experience to be my second-hand, but they can do what I'll ask of them. We're on the ground floor of all this right now, all of us coming here new in some ways. We can all learn and grow together. We have to get this going."

The two Mikes and Claire hesitated but smiled. "OK, Chef," they said at the last meeting before opening on time.

• • •

"Amateur Night went flat on the line now," Dodge said, cleaning up the kitchen counters after we tested a tomato gazpacho with large chunks of watermelons and a dollop of crème fraîche in the center for the grand-opening course on

Valentine's Day. "Ms. Devil in Prada Heels sent that away right along the tracks of its own wings." Dodge's left hand, trying to wave goodbye, curled down like the letter C before crumbling onto itself. "Or we had previously presumed," he continued, spatula clanging on the stovetop, "because good news from out of *that*. And we sure know Ms. Devil Tower in Prada Heels didn't parlay up the eyes to it. Why would she…all standing up in the paint-bin and color-chip remains and Travertine tile of her 'vision'?"

"Who?" I asked Birch sorting knives next to me.

"Ms. Sarsgaard," he whispered with the smell of freshly chopped onions drifting between us.

Dodge joked that the fisherman on the bag of fish sticks during the Wildcats days knew him "like peanut butter lays down a soft song to jelly." He sighed and wiped his hands on towels worn from our practices. "I know I can't register whether or not to have such an incomplete picture of what I am to become, all in accounted for that brought us to this point in the timeline of where we stand now." Dodge blinked, sprinkled salt on a cutting board, grabbed a salmon, and tapped the side of his head. "If I'm staying put with all the stops, then I want. I just."

• • •

The two brothers did not live on the side of the river near Velvet Glove, and they couldn't live anywhere else. The prices across the river had climbed too high. They couldn't rent, nor could they could own without help. Neither of them was capable of working at the technology and Internet firms sprouting in the renovated buildings surrounding VG, Birch explained one day while blanching spinach. He said that, at nine in the morning, Monday through Saturday, they took the number seven from Riverside Station, where they sat patiently under a metal-and-steel awning. A blue television screen hanging from the ceiling of the station listed the bus numbers, routes, and timetables. Birch said green was in-transit, yellow arriving in the next five minutes, red departing. If there was a delay or some kind of impediment to the bus, the route, or the time, a little pixilated worker wearing a hardhat took his broom and swept away the bus number, the route, and the times. A zero with a diagonal line struck through it bounced behind him once he left the screen, past the minutes, followed by the phrase in big font ATTENTION RIDERS. The digitized worker wiped his forehead and put his hardhat back on before being called to duty on some other line on the screen.

The blue screen and the little pixelated man with his gear fascinated Dodge, Birch told me, but Birch couldn't care less, and Dodge, Birch went on while we marked off the space for the new herb garden out back, was infatuated with this that he often wanted to arrive early at the bus station, stand outside the main window, where some of the monitors faced, and stare at the monitors, hoping for such a display—not that Dodge wanted anyone to be hurt or any bus to be in serious danger. Dodge wanted something small to bring out the little pixelated man and his broom and zero with the line slashed into it.

• • •

"Some things peel right down with ways they've made to be apart without having much effort on the other side," Dodge said as he, Birch, and I unloaded the crates I picked up from a ranch on the outskirts of the county. "That's pretty close to what Lonnie says before the lights go out each and every night, and for that I can't disagree."

"Lonnie?" I asked Birch.

"Lonnie and Jamie," he answered, closing my car's trunk. "Our middle brother and his wife. We're with them."

"Birchy and me now get to hold on down to here with each other," Dodge sang on his way back, helping with the arugula salad and setting out pear wedges and a jar of honey. "We both stand up with paychecks here now. We both stood up here with paychecks when it was cast about town in a much alternated image then named Velvet Glove."

I nodded, finished our list for the evening, and showed the brothers what needed to be done. The kitchen's new appliances and utensils sparkled in the morning light. Food-storage bins were coordinated. They had done a fantastic job organizing everything we used or would use.

"But it is now to be forever called Wildcats by those in-house and those paying onsite for its premises. Birchy stood up with a paycheck here first, but now I'm on the slice-dice-and-plate line, this being a long rearview appreciation of when I stood at the front under the moniker of *the* assistant to *the* bouncer. But those days are, on account of what I said, past the windows of the city in the rearview." He paused to look at me before jumping his tired eyes to the stack of onions. "You kept me on because I jump roped all those of your tests…shuttle-cone drills and hot-coal walks. Birchy too, and he was Mr. Pablo Picasso when it was time for that to be his hands and all."

Birch smiled at me and took his time to look over the list each brother had to accomplish. As he had been doing, he suggested a change or two, asked some questions, and dove into work.

"Birchy, got that one from said back there?" Dodge asked.

"You better believe I do," he answered his brother.

"I have been prior to in the kitchen on the slice-dice-and-plate line for near about fifteen stand-alone years, save for that exception of a few weeks when I had to go to the doctor for those gray-matter head-splitters, which on account of my breaking-and-making-records days as a career starter in a 4-3 Renegade defense whiteboard scheme at Lee High seemed to have wanted to tag along, having shimmied up a chance to do so, so what I repeated were flashbacks from kickoff-bursts and goal-line citadels from our long-standing rival with Adair High coming back to say, 'Hi, it's Senior Night. See your parents in the grand seats for that last clock-down run?'"

As we chopped and spiced, Birch said, "Tell us, Dodgey, tell us."

"Don't hold back on us," I caroled.

"Well," he continued, jutting his jaw out, "at first they were certain that it was that *USA Today Sports* reporters have been talking about, making all kinds of unqualified experts worry and putting on so many flags and warning bumper-stickers they made many some panics, and just as I was hitting the big upcoming five-zero-seven. *Five-zero-seven.*" Dodge paused to examine the filets sitting in their wine sauce. "Nonetheless, none of our family branches toss funnies around like bags in an airport collection service department when it comes to the numbers on a birth certificate. Every day…*every day*…is a day of breaths, and due on that, we say, however, how very thankful we are, have been, and will be with those numbers on our birth certificates, because, otherwise there'd be no light to see when the clouds of a dark, dark day puff on over from Gloom and Doom Land, all thanks, we honestly feel, to the many methods our flag-wearing leaders, red and blue, have journeyed us into. And the greenback many-fingers aren't helping."

"Money *is* the root of all evil," I responded out loud.

"Greenback many-fingers is definitely not helping," Birch repeated. "Especially when they're tied to the red and blue flag-wearing leaders."

"We all could use a little sunlight in a bottle," Dodge picked back up, "like David the Giant Killer and Sheepherder had on that envelope slicing open underneath him that day when all of the land had a brightness to it when he said, 'Yes, I will' to that Power above."

Birch pulled out the thick gloves for dry ice. I crossed Dessert from my list. Spring was around the corner, and lamb was available at the farmers' market. Birch waited until Dodge moved a sack of sweet potatoes and walked toward the freezer. He didn't break his rhythm of stirring the boiling stew and said plainly to me, "All those days of playing football."

"Was he good?" I asked.

"The best."

• • •

Days later, Dodge glanced at my wrist, waited until the two of us stood inside the doorway of the kitchen's back door, sprigs of rosemary popping in the garden in front of us, and gently touched the top of my wrist, his hands trembling. I turned it over and rubbed the Mars tattoo and the script underneath.

"Hardheaded. Self-reliant," I told him.

He looked at me and hummed in agreement. "Leather."

"Don't you know that by now?" I teased him.

"On it," he confirmed, flexing his scrawny biceps.

Dodge revealed hours later, tapping above his ear, "My favorite passages before all this at this now was all about the vast space not filled with much out there, but those flashes and rings and specks. Maybe water on there, too. Red Planet. All my favorite, one anyway such as that."

I wiped flour from my sweaty head and looked at Dodge's eyes fading like an old watercolor's blue sky. "Yeah, same here," I said to him. "I liked the magazine *NASA Jr.* when I was younger."

"Oh now, settle here!" He chuckled. "Ms. Dr. Carl Sagan over here all about outer-space graphs and ballistic dimensions."

"That's right. Planets and stars and galaxies. I can name the order of planets in our solar system. And I know Pluto is no longer classified as a planet. Poor Pluto," I pouted.

Grinning widely, Dodge turned up his accent and his volume. "*That* dot." He clenched his eyes before opening them. "Now, I would on the account of being right when I can suspect the Matthew McConaughey would indeed play me in a movie were my life to be filmed up and available for a download here or there with the appropriate amount of exchange value, all thanks to a password I can't offer." He smirked at me before laughing so hard he had to clear his throat. "Set yourself down to the planetarium out here?" he asked, washing his hands and returning to his tasks.

"I didn't know there was one."

"We should up on there sometime."

"We should up on there sometime. That'd be nice."

"Friends," he said, smiling at me. "Not wanting with anything else. Just sit under the stars as two good people. I'm on my way to get somebody in my life, but I am certain that cannot be because of my supervisor Chef. Double Mikes and Ms. C.S. would have a big roll of fair tickets to remember with that."

I laughed. David Bowie, Ziggy Stardust and the Spiders from Mars, I thought under the kitchen's track-lighting of many little full moons. All those oddities fallen to and foreign on Earth —stuck here. Where else?

• • •

Over the first quarter, things moved along so well that management wanted to add a Sunday brunch and show. Birch, Dodge, and I attacked the possibilities and ended up with some pleasing options, including fresh hollandaise sauce on poached quail eggs next to two slices of toast packed with fresh jam and, on the crust, pumpkin seeds and sunflower seeds from the garden fueled by a compost pile that steamed whenever Dodge pulled the cover back. We watched from the kitchen as happy patrons—a mixed bag of young and old, tall and short, thin and thick—packed the front of the house like management's business plan had anticipated. At the back of the house, we joked that most of the men out there had handlebar mustaches, skinny jeans, and undercut hairstyles, and that, the two brothers added, most of the women looked like gypsies filtered through the 1970s. But we didn't care who filled the seats and ate our food, as long as they did and as long as every one of us employed there kept up our standards. Money, media coverage, and check-ins on phones doubled, tripled, but my staff remained a solid core.

By summer, orders started returning to the kitchen.

"And?" I snapped.

"Customer says it's overcooked," one runner said.

"Missing leeks on this, Chef," said another.

"Potato gnocchi on this one."

Birch became quiet and pressed his weight onto his hands flattened on the counter. He tried not glancing at his brother and tightened his lips when he did.

"How can that be tied when it's stopped by being untied?" Dodge stuttered and lunged at the dishes, growling at them each time the runners appeared with half-eaten or uneaten foods pushed and dragged around the earth-toned sauces or left untouched on the plates balanced on the runners' arms.

"Come on, guys! Come on! This isn't us," I boiled. "No more *on the house*, OK? Let's go! Come on!"

We worried the patrons stared at our meltdowns in the open-space kitchen. Management looked our way, too.

Dodge showed up later and later to work, his brother saying he missed the bus, sometimes on accident, sometimes on purpose, and he would be in later, when his head was clear and he could walk in a straight line. And when Dodge showed up, he missed orders, missed the small things that had made him seem different and full of potential. He rambled more and more about his headaches. He rambled about the haze in his head and the haze running over his eyes, sometimes, Birch explained to me, feeling pain behind his eyes, along those wires attaching the back of his eyes to his head. And at five-foot-eleven, Dodge dropped to 120 pounds and walked and talked slower. He prattled about Claire and what she had done to the kitchen and the work atmosphere, to him and Birch, and to the rest of the staff—but mainly to him. Birch thought everything had been rearranged or turned unfamiliar to his older brother while everyone around him had remained stable.

I thought maybe Dodge was in a funk and would turn himself around or Birch would help him out. The two Mikes and Claire wanted it fixed. There was more at stake, but they never specified. "It's your crew, but you may want to reevaluate who's on it. Q3 is coming up. It's a good time to do that before the year ends."

I thought about cutting back Dodge's hours, but to do so would put more pressure on the rest of us and would jeopardize the comings and goings between us—those orbits we had achieved. Birch told me Dodge wouldn't appear to take it personally, but deep down he would. I thought there was a difference between him and his work. I thought there some permanence was in place. I never thought he would worsen.

• • •

Dodge has a gun, I said to myself that day in September. He has a gun, and he's done something horrific to himself or to the dancers or to Claire, and he made sure that whatever horror he did was at VG. Today is the day he has shown up with a gun. We all saw the signs—yes, now in hindsight. And we saw it coming—yes, in hindsight—but we did nothing to help him or to stop it. He wasn't angry about anything the day before, but his head had been tripping so frequently on his confusion—on himself. Police cars, lights on, lined the street in front of the club. A few officers spoke into radios on their shoulders, and a few kept their hands on their holsters. A fire truck with its crew waited behind the line of police, and two EMTs popped open the doors to an ambulance when I pulled in.

A news truck rolled in when I parked my car and got out. I could imagine Dodge saying, in his way, he wasn't sure why he was there with the gun, but he was going to use it. I quickly realized how wrong I was.

"Something went out," Birch said, wiping his face with a towel and sitting on the ambulance's bumper. "We showed up early to get in all that work we missed. He said he felt good today, best he had in a long time. That's why he wanted to get here early…to surprise you and, I think, even Ms. Sarsgaard. He starting grinding the coffee beans and…he slumped over and fell."

Birch said Dodge was a few months shy of turning fifty-seven. Five-zero-seven.

• • •

Traffic on the downtown streets three floors below is quiet on a Sunday afternoon, 3:33 central time. The spring and summer storm seasons have moved on, the violent air come and gone. The sky is blue and cloudless, and the tips of leaves are starting to turn into the colors of fall. And it's that end-of-the-weekend quiet, and I know plenty of recliners in this town are kicked back and tables are cluttered with plates and silverware and soiled napkins from large meals, and it's that everyone-with-family-and-friends kind of quiet typically cast in movies, paintings, or photographs or evoked when the theme calls for uncongested tranquility in the America and Americans far from coastal big cities.

My phone rings. It could be my parents. This time on Sundays is their window to call before they have a late dinner and watch an old movie—a classic they've seen in the past and want to see again before, as Dad has said, "Hollywood ruins it by remaking it." I haven't told them anything about the past week yet. They will want to be with me. I watch the phone vibrate. It could be Birch calling, who, before he went fishing to get his mind off things, was waiting to hear from the medical examiner. The ME was supposed to deliver the autopsy results before the end of Friday. Yesterday I practiced saying, "I know I was a demanding boss, and I know I was in charge, and I know he struggled toward the end, especially when we all were under pressure to perform. I'm sorry." It felt inauthentic to me, but it was a kind of exorcism in between bouts of tears, memories, and judgments. At this point I don't know which is worse—avoiding my parents or having to talk to Birch about Dodge and how he died.

A breeze carries the aroma of rosemary, sends it over the wood floor of my patio, and drifts down onto some cars parking on the street and entering the building's garage on the ground floor. I can't determine if the aroma has drifted from the planters on my balcony or I've imagined the door between VG's kitchen and the garden out back has momentarily walled me in. My neighbor's TV flicks on. His windows are open, and a game whistle blasts a few times before he switches to a radio station and its advertisement for T-Town Pizza and Wings, after which the program returns to Get the Led Out – All Zep, All Sunday Afternoon on 97.1 Classic Rock. The opening guitar riff to "Ramble On" jangles. The phone quiets before buzzing three quick bursts. The new voicemail icon blinks. I scold myself. The sun lowers a little more on my walls and brightens as it does. The old converted warehouse's brick is a jagged, crimson landscape.

After listening to the voicemail, I call back. The phone's screen blinks RICHARD PRITCHETT. It used to say MOM & DAD, but I read that criminals, if they steal your phone and if they crack its passcode, scroll through your list of contacts, looking for the big give-away names, such as PARENTS, SPOUSE, GRANDPARENTS, AUNTY-UNCLE, BIG BRO, and give them a ring with nasty bait on the end. "I'm calling on behalf of ______. There's been a horrible accident, and ______ is in serious trouble and needs money/personal information/address/account to get out of it. ______ wanted me to call you because it's the one chance we have to get hold of you."

My parents' number glows, and I hold the phone and wait for them to answer. I don't have anything to say right away. I have no words to cast or to lure them in. And I can't help but imagine the scenario, the other line chiming, "Hello, Eva? Eva, it's your mother. Dick, why isn't she answering?" "Evey-girl," Dad would jump in, "are you there? Bad connection maybe. Evey?" And I can see Mom in the living room cradling the chipped, off-white cordless phone I used when living there decades ago, while Dad sits in the kitchen chair holding the yellow landline phone—but both of them are on the line at the same time.

We'll start with the simple questions. Weather in Tulsa as compared to where they live (little to no difference). Family updates (who's died, who's infirm, who's not talking to whom on account of a quip or a slight and, as a result, names being changed on wills). Church will be mentioned—the one they recently started attending ("less about theology and more about community," which, Mom said several Sundays ago, they need now in their retirement years). Dad will add a few yes's and no's on the phone from his spot in the kitchen and keep his news short and sweet (save for his distaste for the current state of the union, no matter who's in charge).

"How's the job going, honey?" they will ask.

Together, the weight and I will tell them—one of us pulling the long string of what has happened, like a puppet and its puppeteer tied together; one of us sitting and listening; one of us doing all the talking. But I won't mention my recent dreams— of going to an observatory, of arriving under a fully illuminated planet, a bright red circle in a sea of black—waking me the past few nights.

In one dream, I walked outside. The line to the main telescope was too long, so I peered through some of the telescopes fastened along the handrail. The planet grew darker, redder, and heavier the more I turned my attention to it—the details of its surface. Stars filled the sky above like a slowly projected film. How is my dream so specific for a thing so far away? I wondered. But as a chunk of alien rock, sand, and wind-carved canyons, even as a dream, it whispered nothing to me; it uttered nothing; it asked nothing of me. It was no oracle. It offered no guidance, no solace. It hovered in the middle of my head, in the middle of my dream. It seemed as though it had waited for me, waited for a moment to be with me, and had found that moment. How else could I have asked for it?

Wish You Were Here

Now, this young woman, this Greta, said she was his daughter, and her last name not matching up with Bill's didn't mean she wasn't. From a glance, she looked like him in profile, which is what I thought while I made sure the blowtorch was off. She had broken up the shoot because she had to see him, but she didn't say why, at least with all of us standing there, or that her interruption was on purpose, like an announcement planned in advance. But she had broken up the shoot by accident, and given the confusion on her face, she was lucky and, to some degree, so it seemed, lost in the city with its crisscrosses and neighborhoods, that she didn't know what she had stumbled into but somehow knew Bill was back there and pleaded enough somehow with security and the lot manager to let her make it that far onto the property, somehow knew to walk through the studio, past the green room where we had been, running by that point probably because security and the lot manager were chasing after her, and by chance ended up where we had set up for the shot. All Bill knew up to that point was he was on fire.

The big man didn't show to her or to any of us there he was buying it—that she was his daughter—but something else too about his reaction, which was a long stare at her while he stood there under the flames, was letting us know he was buying it, it didn't surprise him at all, and she was his daughter, was blood, and not telling a lie to get herself backstage, behind the scenes at the movies or in one, which our set-up was no place for that because we're behind the scenes in a different way even if some of us, like Bill but not us crew, were on the screen.

But there she was, not more than twenty years old, having come out of the door from the green room that dumped her and all that indoor studio light into the alleyway—this Greta in her red flat-soled sneakers and jeans ripped at the knees, flowery white shirt of hers falling down to the denim threads barely covering her knees, and this young woman causing too much artificial light to be there in that narrow space supposed to be filled only with shadows, the late-morning sun, and the two men standing there—one of which was Bill ready to stick his hand out and shake Danny's hand, his partner for the shoot, while flames curled on his body.

The lot manager had knocked on the green room's door when we were in there several minutes ago and helping Bill get ready by slathering the gel on his skin, especially his cheeks and neck, some areas of his wig, and spots on his jacket, especially near the collar and cuffs, where I would apply the blowtorch, before he put on the bodysuit and topped that with the shirt, tie, and suit picked out by the art director. Danny was ready to go and lounged on a plush leather sofa at the back of the room, his hair styled perfectly like a sculpture—no wig for him, no direct fire for him. He wore a suit, with its blue the color of the ocean when it's halfway to the horizon and no sun setting in it, which the art director picked out when we showed the results of some of us on crew having hit a few department and thrift stores in the area. The studio wardrobe's department did not want us using anything they had, especially if we planned on going through suits to get the right shot. I assumed they'd at least give us some used moth-eaten stuff. Bill sat in the silver chair that used to belong in a barbershop. He sat there in his robe and black socks pulled up to his shins like a man waiting for a shave early in the morning. His suit was ashen-gray.

The doorknob rattled, but we couldn't unlock it because our hands were covered in the fire-retardant gel. We saved Bill's right hand for last because it was the key area we had to concentrate on. His right hand would be on fire. But the knocking and the door rattling kept on, and one of us—it was Wayne Hernandez—grabbed a towel and opened the door.

We must have been a sight to the lot manager who looked for Bill, looked around the room at five men, four of them with shiny, slick hands, and one man zipping his pants, wearing a curly black wig, and his right hand gleaming in the lamps.

But the lot manager had no sense of any humor that morning. "Bill, there's a young woman out front asking for you. Says she's your daughter."

We glanced at each other and then at Bill who turned his left ear to the door and barely looked over there because of the bodysuit, the wig, and the jacket slowing him down. He knotted the black tie up to the shirt's white collar, the rest of the shirt a gray-blue. We had bundled him so his moves were simple and straightforward and, more importantly, so he was well protected. This wasn't going to be a multi-sequence action shot, but it was one of the most dangerous ones we had done with Bill in the years working together.

The former linebacker from Kentucky kept quiet, and we gave him space to respond to the lot manager who wanted an answer. But the big man barely moved in the chair. After several seconds of silence he asked, "What's her name?"

"Greta…something. Not Radinsky."

We all kept looking at Bill rotating his shoulders inside his jacket and up to his earlobes slicked with fire-retardant gel. He nodded his chin, with its scar shaped like a river outlining a border, and asked us if he was ready to go. When we said yes, he asked one of us to help him with the loafers he couldn't tie because everything under the suit tightened his skin, and if anything cracked because he moved the wrong way or too quickly, he didn't want to have to sit through this all over again.

We all looked at Wayne because his hands were wiped clean, and Wayne tied the loafers and joked he was not going to help the stuntman with his pants again, which Bill laughed in return and double-checked his zipper. He commented on how polished his loafers were—that those shoes for work were polished better than the scuffed steel-toed boots he wore on his wedding day. "I clean up pretty good when I have to," he joked, catching his reflection in the mirror, adjusting the pocket square, and turning his squat face left to right.

"Bill?" the lot manager interrupted, "I can tell her you're in the middle of a shoot."

But Bill didn't hear the lot manager, probably because by that time we had dipped the wig in some of the gel and wrangled it onto his head, over the bodysuit's hood, adding some more gel once the wig was in place because that was going to be a hot spot where I would lay the blowtorch.

The lot manager mumbled something after saying, "I'll take a message," turned, and headed toward the door from the green room into the lobby.

We pulled Bill out of the chair and surrounded him like a parade float, but he kept clopping along, no problems at all. With his non-gelled hand, Danny opened the door leading out of the green room and into the alleyway between that studio and the one across from it. The late-morning light had started filling the alley, and the photographer was ready to shoot, having told us there were two windows to do this. We were in the first window available between ten and noon, and after the gloom of summer fog burned off, the light would brighten the alleyway. The second window was mid-afternoon, sometime between two and four. The day would be the brightest, but because the sun was headed toward the ocean, the light in the alleyway would be similar to the morning's light. "A well-lit space," the photographer had said.

But neither of those windows mattered when all was said and done because what mattered more was the wind. The light and the shadows were important, and getting Bill and Danny to shake hands quickly was also important, but one quick burst of wind could jeopardize the shoot and the stuntmen. The smallest breeze could pull flames in other directions. Fire and wind were not the best partners to pair up. The weather that summer had been typical—bright, moderate days; wind closer to the ocean than inland. But we couldn't take any chances. The alleys between the studios on the lot collected wind like city streets. And we also had to complete this project. The label execs, the art director, and the photographer wanted images for the album cover long before the September release. The results fell on us.

Once the door from the green room to the alleyway opened, we could see the two X's the photographer's assistant had taped on the concrete. The lot manager had blocked out the calendar for this shoot and had the facilities crew place barriers and signs—AREA CLOSED FOR FILMING UNTIL FURTHER NOTICE.

The camera had been set up a few feet from the pieces of white tape. Bill took his spot on the western X, which placed him on the right when he faced the camera. He inched in enough until the Hollywood Hills couldn't be seen. As soon as Bill rubbed his shoes on the concrete and planted himself, we showed Danny the other X. The two stuntmen chuckled at each other and shook hands without fire. Bill looked over at me and pumped his thumb over his finger-gun. The photographer, the assistant, and the art director talked for a few minutes. They had Bill move a little this way, Danny that way. They moved the camera. They tilted the umbrella shades. They eventually got rid of the shades and let the light and the shadows of the City of Angels take over. They liked what they saw, the two men lined up, the alleyway shrinking behind them and disappearing under the baby-blue sky, all of this framed by the cream-colored studios stacked along the path. The two men stepped off their respective X's and returned after the photographer's assistant peeled up the tape. The art director was adamant about the slacks and the loafers of both men being visible "in the deal."

While I unpacked the blowtorch and a fuel canister, the photographer and art director had the stuntmen practice dry. First, Bill moved to Danny, and the big rectangle of a stuntman held his arm out the whole time. Danny moved to Bill, and the art director had Bill wait until Danny was closer to offer his hand. The art director was a short man, most of his weight in the belly. He had a heavy British accent and wore all white—white short-sleeve shirt, white belt, white pants that stopped short of his ankles—and said, pointing to Danny, "No, no, no. Have the glad-hander extend *his* hand for the shake. But they come together as one." Pointing to Bill, he said, "He has the briefcase. It makes sense." He watched their handshake a few times and asked for the briefcase to be taken away. He wanted "less props" and more attention on the "body language of the suits." He told both stuntmen to put on sunglasses.

We were ready for the shoot. The photographer reminded us that, once *Action!* was yelled, the camera would click on multi-shutter, and no one should stop the movement unless Bill or Danny called out or one of us on the stunt crew noticed something awry with the fire. We confirmed we had the fire extinguishers nearby and went to our assigned spots.

After priming the fuel line, I started the blowtorch. I had set things on fire, but I had never set a man on fire. I had pushed them off building ledges, shot at them with rifles and pistols, and drowned them in water.

We had to be quick and on our toes, but out of everybody on crew, I had to move the fastest. Danny had to stand there and wait, and Wayne double-checked the fire-retardant gel on his receiving hand, in case the flames jumped. I walked up to

Bill and let him know I was going to start on his shoulder because it was the biggest area for the fire—and if things went wrong at that point, we could cancel the stunt without putting him at too much risk. I would move down his arm and finish up with his right hand. And if things were still A-OK at that point, I'd spray the final shot of fire on his wig. Bill could only start the handshake after the fire grew on him, which he would know when the photographer's assistant cued him.

The big man gave a verbal confirmation to me, which I delivered as a thumbs-up to the rest of the crew.

"Light him up!" the assistant yelled.

The flames ripped off like orange and yellow book covers and flapped around Bill's suit. And that was when two things happened at once—one, it seemed, anticipating the other before it happened, like watching pebbles and dirt dribble down a steep slope.

Bill hesitated with his handshake. He stopped moving. He's usually the last one to quit, and we have to pry him from the stunt after the cameras stop. He turned his body toward the door. There was nobody there, but the way he stood made it seem like there was. The photographer yelled at him to turn the other way. But he didn't. Seconds ticked by, and for that stunt, seconds felt like hours. We knew something was up, and by the time we figured the stunt had flopped, Greta burst through the door.

When no handshake appeared, only Danny snapped back his arm. Nobody else moved. Not the photographer or the art director. Not Greta, who didn't scream and couldn't continue any further, blocked by the man in flames who she alleged was her father in front of her and by security and the lot manager catching up behind her. I killed the fuel to the blowtorch and could see the two of them out of the corners of my eyes.

When Bill dropped to his knees and rolled, we pulled the pins on the extinguishers and smothered him with the chemical blankets after he stood still for so long with the fire swirling around him—and stared at Greta staring.

• • •

Phone calls kept coming in that Sunday afternoon a week before the shoot. We were over at Bill's place for drinks and a cookout. The phone on the kitchen wall would rattle—the bell rattling so much it seemed like the phone could fall apart into little green plastic flowers. And then it would fall silent. Minutes later, it would ring again, and we'd look at it and then at Bill. A few of us asked if we could get it, but he'd kept doing whatever he was doing—grilling, chatting with us and the people we brought, and sticking his head back in through the patio door for an update on the Reds-Dodgers game. The rest of the house had maintained its charm. Bill hadn't changed a thing after moving in years ago. Coming home from work, he said, he wanted to sit in the big puffy chair wedged between the back patio and the television, a cold beer on his knee, and maybe someday soon a dog by his side. The phone wasn't hard to miss. It was avocado green in a canary-yellow kitchen. He refused to answer it.

During the middle of the fifth, the Boys in Blue were down three runs and their best pitcher, who was still a rookie in many ways and who had already insulted his teammates during interviews, was not in fine form. The hometown crowd booed when he stepped on the mound.

Bill had been a lifelong Reds fan, but when he moved out here, he told us he wanted to be part of the scene, his new life having sprung from a fabrication factory buried in the Cumberland Gap. He wanted to be here and nowhere else. A lot of us could relate. Most of us on the stunt crew had relocated for different reasons. Some of us had been born and bred here. He and JoAnne were newly married, she being from Santa Monica, where they lived in an apartment cramped for space but less than five minutes from the Pacific. Seeing the Pier at sunset, he said, the sun sinking into the ocean, reds and purples spreading across the sky, beat the flashing lights and casino noises of Vegas any day of the week. Bill told us swimming in the Pacific was like standing next to an oven compared to freezing in a lake.

His wife wasn't with him anymore. He spoke about JoAnne in a way we could connect the dots. It wasn't surprising. The war had ended, a new president had taken over, and plenty of marriages and families and relationships were taking a hit from what had happened. The war had been nasty. There were protests then, and there were still protests about something, almost daily. People were heated. A lot of talk about who was right, who was wrong, and what was to be done. JoAnne and Bill, they found out, had different views, and they stopped pretending to hide their differences. The marriage went on until it couldn't divide anymore or be put back together.

They had split, Bill said, on good terms that most couples going through rough patches, and eventually the final days, would envy. There were no yelling matches, throwing objects, or packing suitcases while the other person was at work. Neither Bill nor JoAnne came home to an empty house and a note explaining what, when, and why but not where, as in *where to next*—where everything had been up to that point and where everything would end up. They said their goodbyes face to face, JoAnne having waited for Bill to come home and told him what he already knew and what they had accepted in secret but had not brought into the light. And then the door to their small apartment closed, he said.

JoAnne had stopped by, once, after he moved to the Valley. This wasn't too long ago. Bill had told her where he lived and when to stop by, if she wanted, which he told us he was only being polite, not encouraging it. He didn't think she would, but there she was, standing on his old doormat, one of the few things he had brought with him after the separation. He said he wasn't getting back together with her. He didn't see any reason. It was the job he wanted, not much else. He didn't know what she wanted.

He asked her what brought her to town, and she was off and running with a series of questions for which he had no answers. He thought she had something to tell him but never did. He told her about the new gig that could be a defining moment for him—not a movie but an album cover for a rock 'n' roll band. "You know them, but I can't say." She wasn't happy with his response. "Oh, God, Bill. There's so much more than that these days."

We knew the band. Bill did, too. We all had listened to them on the radio but never went out of our way to buy any of their albums. We didn't dislike them, like we did with some of the other bands clumped together with them, but we also didn't consider them someone we'd beat ourselves up over if we never heard them live. There were worse bands, and there were better bands. Being able to work at what we did seemed more important.

The next batter smacked a two-run double into right field. The ball spun in a corner of the center-right wall until the outfielder fired it to the second baseman. Safe. The Dodgers rookie pitcher had been smoked again.

The ringing spaced out until minutes became hours. Before the get-together was over, the phone rang one last time, and Bill answered it like someone opening a door after knocks strung together a kind of message. He stood in the kitchen in his butterfly-collar shirt and corduroy jeans. He had dressed up for his own party. He turned away from us, crossed his arms, and lowered his head. "Where are you now?" we heard him ask the ghost on the other end. There was a hope and happiness lifting his voice nobody had heard before. We were all, it seemed, due for a little hope and happiness. It was, after all, night, and it was 1975.

• • •

No charges were pressed once things cleared up with security and the studio. But the album cover changed. Not the concept—the handshake was still there, the men in suits, the studio backdrop, the fire, the image saying so much without having to say anything at all. But after what happened, Bill didn't make the cut, and he helped the execs decide when he didn't show up the next day.

We saw him roll into the parking lot that morning, sit in his car, long past the time he was supposed to check in before he drove away. Another stuntman took his place. He had to, or else we'd all be out of a job and word would spread about us. We went through the steps all over again but with someone different.

The new stuntman was good, a hard worker who listened to what was needed. We had worked with him before. He was as professional as Bill. The fire ate through his jacket and dress shirt, and we could see the bodysuit underneath the burned holes. A surprise breeze singed Ronald's mustache and sideburns—*his* mustache and sideburns, not hairpieces glued on. We got what we needed in less time than we budgeted. The man on fire could have been anybody who was willing to stand there, endure it, and be paid for it. It was Bill for a little bit. It was someone else in the end.

Some of us saw Bill a few times after the shoot. They said he was the same in some ways but much happier in other ways. He knew about his replacement but didn't say much about the cover other than "good luck" and to make sure we got it done in time, which we did. He said he was looking for work but wouldn't be disappointed if nothing panned out. He said he had other options and knew in his own way those options would find him.

I heard he met his daughter in a proper way, without all the dangers of a stunt blowing up around them, without someone else's money and property on the line. Some things like that never happen for some people, but for Bill it did.

They were at a museum, of all places. One of the crew's girlfriends worked there, and he was there one day and saw Bill. He was sure it was the big man. This being Tommy Martino, he said he was with his girlfriend and saw Bill in the main gallery on the second floor filled with paintings, some large, some small, but all from Spanish painters dating from the last few decades to way, way back. Tommy said Bill wore that one suit and tie he had—his own—not like the silky ones he wore in the shoot. Tommy said Greta looked like a flower with the red sneakers on her feet and a cap of wild black hair like Bill's. Tommy said he stayed back and didn't want to interfere with them. They looked happy.

He said Bill adjusted his tie and walked into the gallery. His boots clacked on the tile, and some guests looked over at him when he entered. Greta was already there, waiting, reading a book, and rose to meet him when she saw him. They didn't hug. They didn't cry or laugh. No handshake. They looked at each other and smiled like someone receiving a postcard from far away.

They started at the religious paintings—the ones of the Holy Mother and Child and then onto the Gospels, the Acts of the Disciples, and Paul writing his letters from prison. Greta doubled back to one tall painting of the Crucifixion with Christ's pale body and the cross being the only colors in a sea of black, nothing else there, Tommy said. She met up with Bill at a painting of two men squaring off and swinging cudgels over their heads. The last one they took their time at was at a brightly colored piece with a family of circus performers and white horses.

I saw them at one of the busiest DMVs in the area. Now, this was pretty recent. They were stuffed in the line with everybody else and their documents. Most everyone there had triple digits stamped on their slips while the counter on the wall clicked off double digits. But Bill and Greta stood there, laughing every now and then, which was funny to hear because Bill hated long lines, avoided them every chance he could. He would grumble when he would see the line at the studio's cafeteria during lunch break.

But the two of them crept along, the number counter buzzing, the next person ahead of them in line moving to one window, only to be told to go to another window or return with the proper papers, which meant starting all over again at the back of the line. None of this slow pace seemed to bother Greta. She smiled the whole time. Bill seemed to enjoy it, too, even if being there took all day.

ACKNOWLEDGMENTS

Many thanks to the following publications where versions of stories in *A Fine Day Will Burn Through* first appeared:

"Corporate Games," *Thoughtful Dog*

"Crane and Hoist," *BULL*

"Fog," *museum of americana*

"FOMO," *The McNeese Review*

"Many and Many A Year Ago," 2019 Norton Girault Literary Prize in Fiction, *Barely South Review*

"Martingale," *Slush Pile Magazine*

"Rail Time," *Gravel*

"Start of the Season," *Valparaiso Fiction Review*

"Sun on Snow on Mountains," finalist, 2019 Great Midwest Writing Contest, *Midwest Review*

"Transplant," *Open: Journal of Arts & Letters*

And to everyone who reads and supports me and my work—thank you. I'll see you soon.

ABOUT THE AUTHOR

William Auten is the author of the novels *In Another Sun* (2020, Tortoise Books) and *Pepper's Ghost*, a 2017 Eric Hoffer Award finalist for contemporary fiction. His work has appeared widely online and in print. williamauten.com.